THE BET

A NOVEL

 Faith

CHIRLEY ROUNDY ARNOLD

A S P E N
B O O K S

Titles in the *Values for Young Women Series*

Faith—*The Bet* by Chirley Arnold
Divine Nature—*Amaryllis Lilies* by Marcie Gallacher
Choice & Accountability—*Butterfly Dust* by Kathryn Palmer

The Bet
© 1997 by Chirley Arnold
All rights reserved.
Printed in the United States.

No portion of this book may be reproduced in any form
without written permission from the publisher,
Aspen Books, 6200 S. Stratler, Murray, UT 84107

Library of Congress Cataloging-in Publication Data

Arnold, Chirley
    The Bet / Chirley Arnold
        p.   cm. -- (Values for young women)
        Summary: When Julie's mother is diagnosed with cancer and decide
move the family back to Utah, Julie gives up her chance to study at Julliard, but
her boyfriend that she will not join the Mormon Church.
        ISBN 1-56236-450-2 (pbk.)
        [1. Mormon--Fiction. 2. Family life--Fiction.] I. Title. II. Series.
    PZ7. A7348Be 1996
    [Fic]--dc20   96-20483
                                                       CIP
                                                       AC

10 9 8 7 6 5 4 3 2 1

Dedication

To my husband, Doug,
who is enthusiastic about my writing
and continually encouraging.
To my daughter, Sarah,
who says this is her favorite book.

CHAPTER ONE

The Bet

Good Mormons don't bet. I know that now, but at the time I wasn't a Mormon.

Before the bet, my mother was the only connection I had with the Church. Her parents, Grandpa and Grandma Willis, were members, and so were Uncle Bill and his family. They lived in Utah, but they weren't a part of my life. Utah was Hicksville. I didn't associate with hicks for any longer than I could help it back then. I never really got to know Mom's side of the family until the doctor gave his final opinion. What he told Mom changed her whole perspective on life. It eventually changed mine, too.

There we were, a nice modern family unit, consisting of me, my younger brother, Theodore, and my mom and dad. We lived in New York City—Trump Towers to be exact. My dad was doing very well in business. You can tell by the address. If you've ever ridden the elevator with Sophia Loren, you know what I mean. We had it made.

I had my own special group of friends at school—students whose parents' salaries started in six digits. Some of them experimented a little with marijuana, but I didn't. Drugs messed up their emotions and mushed their plans for the future. At the time, I said no to drugs because of Ruwanda, the baby grand piano my mother and father had given me for Christmas several years before. According to my friends, Ruwanda was my only vice. I spent hours playing Liszt and Chopin.

My future in music was serious business. I was headed for the Juilliard School of Music and nothing was going to stand in my way.

I should have seen it coming back then, just like the progressive notes on a staff. But I didn't. It started with gradual changes in my mother's attitude. She'd say little things like, "When I was your age . . ." even before her illness was diagnosed. I thought reliving the past was just part of her mid-life crisis. But I was wrong.

Before starting my senior year, Mom had insisted I apply to a number of different universities. "You're a great musician, Julie," she said, "and if they don't take you it's their loss, but you can't hang all your hopes on Juilliard. Things happen that can't be foreseen. It's better to be prepared."

So in the spirit of Girl Scouting (my mother had once been one), I sent my application to three other universities in New York and one out to Utah. Brigham Young University was the school my mom had attended before she met my dad. I figured her insistence on BYU was based on sentimentality. When the time came, however, I planned to stay close to home, and that meant New York City and the Juilliard School of Music.

Focusing my attention on my goal, I practiced night and day for my upcoming audition at Juilliard. On the scheduled day, I arrived early to find a long line of competitors. I sat and stared at them, wondering who would be among the chosen few. Would I be accepted? After what seemed like an eternity, I was ushered before the jury. There were seven all together on the panel and not a smile among them.

"Your name, please," droned an austere looking woman in gray.

My mind froze. I had known it before I walked through the door. "Julie," I squeaked.

"We don't have your name on the list, Louise."

"My name's Julie," I said louder. "Julie Edwards."

"Okay, Julie." Her mouth curved into a grimace. "Take a seat at the piano and show us what you've got."

Taking a deep breath, I touched the keys and thought of Ruwanda. I was home in the living room playing my own piano. "Polonaise," one of Chopin's favorites, played forcefully, yet with a light touch. Exhaling, I claimed the keys as my own.

I looked up as I hit the last chord. A faint smile flickered at the corner of the mouth of the woman in gray. That was all, but it felt good. I played my other pieces, gaining more confidence after each one. Bach, Beethoven, Mozart, and for the finale, "The Thunderer" by John Philip Sousa.

As the weeks passed with no answer, I kept reflecting back on the feeling I had as I walked out the door. My audition had gone well in spite of everything. The doubt crept in as I wondered how good the others had been. The only thing to do was wait and see.

Then the bomb fell. Not a tangible one; it didn't physically destroy our lush apartment. Ruwanda was still intact, waiting for my fingers to stroke the keys like gently lapping waves or plummet thunderously like cascading water.

At eighteen, when I was ready to leave behind the immaturities of high school for a higher calling at Juilliard, I didn't need to find out my mother was dying of cancer. That knowledge destroyed the walls I had built up protecting myself against the harsher realities of life. I suddenly realized my mother was vulnerable and that made me vulnerable, too. I had thought I lived a charmed life. I was wrong.

I was in a state of disorientation and Mom made it worse. She decided to return to her roots in Provo, Utah. She said I didn't need to come. I was free to go to Juilliard if I wanted. But Theodore didn't have a choice. Nine was too young. And Dad didn't either. He felt guilty. I could see it in his eyes.

My life was New York, where we had lived as long as I could remember. New York, where Dad's business was booming. Computers had been good to him the last couple of years. As the business skyrocketed, we had moved up with it, changing addresses until we had arrived at Trump Towers two years ago.

New York had it all, including hospitals for chemotherapy treatment. We didn't need to go to the University of Utah for that, but Mom insisted. I think she felt guilty, too. It wasn't until later that I found out why.

A few days before our departure, my boyfriend, Darwin, and I went to watch the Rockettes one last time.

"Where did you say you were going?" Darwin asked. He ran his fingers through his thick blond hair, a small frown tugging at the corners of his mouth.

"Utah."

"Is that near California?"

"It's somewhere in the Rocky Mountains."

"If it's anything like the Blue Ridge Mountains, you'll end up playing country."

His smile was perfectly gorgeous, even if it was in appreciation of his own joke.

Darwin hailed a cab that dropped us at Radio City.

"Good thing I bought our tickets in advance." He took my hand and pushed his way toward the entrance.

The line for those without tickets ended somewhere around the corner. I turned up the collar on my Liz Claiborne jacket. Even in summer New York could be a little chilly.

We found our seats and Darwin twined his fingers with mine. "Mothers are important, Julie, but not as important as Juilliard." His blue eyes met mine, heightening in intensity. "Stay," he begged.

We made a great couple. My long black hair and too-white skin seemed to complement his tanned, muscular body. His membership in the school ski club helped keep him tanned and fit. When he first asked me out the beginning of my senior year, Francine, my best friend, had been jealous. It wasn't until she started dating Dave that our friendship got back on an even keel.

I looked down at my hands. Heaven knows I wanted to stay. I wanted Juilliard and Darwin. But I had an obligation. I owed something I had to repay.

"I can't."

"Utah will suffocate you."

"I can be myself wherever I am."

"Not there—not away from the things you love. You have your music and your life to think about."

"I'm thinking about life, maybe for the first time." I looked up.

"I don't want to lose you." His face drooped and his lips pursed into a pout. That expression was his only weakness.

"What's so special about me?" I asked.

"Well, for starters, you play the piano better than any girl I know."

I smiled and blushed simultaneously.

"My little vain Julie," he laughed.

"I'm not vain," I insisted, feeling my cheeks burn hotter.

Darwin laughed again. "What am I going to do without you?"

His teasing made me angry. "Who are you going to lose me to? A country hick?" I chided.

"Maybe, or maybe you'll go to Utah and become a Mormon."

"What! Me a Mormon?"

"Your parents are Mormon aren't they?"

"Yes, but in name only. They haven't practiced their religion in years."

"Then why has your mother suddenly decided to go back?"

I shrugged. "To see her family."

"I'll bet you become a Mormon," he razzed.

"I won't."

"You will too."

"I will not."

"I'll give you six months."

"Make it eight and I'll still win."

We shook hands as the drum roll signaled the opening of the show. The curtain went up. I caught a whiff of Musk and snuggled as close as the seats allowed against everything that was Darwin.

On the day we left our apartment for good, the letter finally arrived. I was accepted at Juilliard. My dreams had come true, but I couldn't fulfill them. If I did and my mother died, I would never be able to live with myself. I threw the letter in the trash and shut myself in the bathroom. As I stared at the blank walls, an ache welled up inside. Tears spilled unbidden down my cheeks. Why me? Why now? I sank to the floor, heavy with an overpowering feeling of loss. If only I had been rejected.

"Julie, come on. We're late." Theodore pounded on the door.

"Hold the tympani," I yelled. "I'm coming." I wasn't going to look back no matter what. Drying my eyes, I took one last look in the bathroom mirror and closed the door on my old life forever.

CHAPTER TWO

Busy Signal

Grandma and Grandpa Willis met us at the Salt Lake City airport. Grandma's eyes brimmed with tears as she hugged first Mom and then the rest of us. Theodore wiggled away, but I didn't. Grandma's arms held comfort. They generated security and love, making me wonder why we hadn't visited more often in the past.

As we left the airport, Grandpa insisted we move in with them while Mom and Dad house hunted. They had two extra bedrooms going to waste. I looked at Theodore and frowned. Why couldn't it have been three? Two meant that Theodore and I would be together. For Mom's sake I decided to keep my complaints to myself. It was only temporary, anyway.

The first night together as friendly strangers, we ate meatloaf and talked politely, keeping to safe subjects like the weather and school.

Finally Grandma Willis asked, "So your treatment starts tomorrow, Gloria?"

When Mom nodded, she added, "Well, you just take our car. Grandpa can use the truck. Can't you dear?" Grandma patted his hand.

"Can I go, too?" Theodore asked.

"You both can." Dad smiled at me.

It sounded as if we were planning a picnic. That wasn't the way I envisioned the seriousness of Mom's illness at all. Cancer was life-threatening. Chemotherapy seemed to be her only chance.

A nurse walked through the doorway of the waiting room. "Gloria Edwards," she called.

Mom got up too quickly and bumped her leg on the coffee table. "It'll be all right, Mom," I said. Who was I trying to reassure? After she left, the doubts crept in.

I picked up a magazine from the table and flipped through the pages to avoid looking at the grim expression on my father's face. When Mom wasn't around, he let his guard down, and that really scared me.

The magazine pages sailed by until I came to a full-page spread of a telephone. Expecting to read an advertisement for AT&T, I glanced at the caption: "With God you never get a busy signal." What? Turning to the front cover I reread the name of the magazine, *New Era,* published by The Church of Jesus Christ of Latter-day Saints. Mormons were everywhere out here. I set the magazine back on the table.

"Did you find something good, Julie?" Theodore asked.

"No, just a picture of a telephone."

"Let me see." He grabbed the magazine.

I ignored him and stared at the painting on the wall. It was a print of a landscape. At least it evoked the desired effect. It offered the observer a chance to escape from the sterile waiting room to the shade of pine trees. I wondered how familiar I would become with the meandering path through the pines before this ordeal was over.

Mom felt fine on the way home. Just to make sure she stayed that way, Dad made her lie down and rest in their room. He sat by the side of her bed rubbing her forehead and talking in soothing tones. It was obvious I wasn't the only one that needed reassurance she was going to be all right.

In spite of Mom's wishes, I'm sure he would have kept her in New York if he had any doubt about the treatment at the University of Utah. The hospital, however, was on the top of the list for chemotherapy treatment. Dad always liked the best, and the move to Utah was getting the best for Mom.

Saturday morning my fingers began drumming of their own accord. I tapped the first few lines of Beethoven's "Menuetto" on the phone book, switching to Strauss's "Reverie" on a stack of newly dried plates. When the plates tipped over, Grandma sent me down to the chapel to practice. It was a good thing it was close enough to walk, since there was a definite shortage of taxicabs in Provo.

I walked into the foyer and found the piano through the double door to the left, just as Grandma had said. To my amazement, there was an organ in the same room as the piano. I decided to try them both. The organ was so smooth my fingers slipped on the keys. I moved to the piano and started playing the pieces I had performed at the Juilliard tryout. Halfway through the first one, I stopped playing. The music was pulling the scab off the wound I carried inside.

I was retreating across the foyer when I heard a male voice. "I don't suppose you know who was just playing that music by Chopin?"

I spun around, confronting a short, rather plump man. His shirt-sleeves were rolled to his elbows and he cradled a stack of papers in the crook of his arm.

"That was me," I stammered. "Is something wrong?" I reached behind me, groping for the bar to open the outside door. "My grand-mother, Mrs. Willis, sent me down here to practice."

"So, you're Sister Willis's granddaughter." He juggled the papers to his left side and shook my hand. "You're welcome here, anytime. I'm Bob Roberts. Where did you learn to play like that?"

"In New York. With Ruwanda," I added, and then wished I hadn't. No one knew I called my piano Ruwanda.

"Was that your teacher?"

"A friend." I looked vaguely over his shoulder.

"I'm the ward choir director. If you sing half as well as you play, you'll be a great asset to the group."

"Thanks, but I don't think so. I don't know how long we're going to be here."

"I thought your Grandmother told me you were moving out here."

"We are, but you see, my mother's sick and we just don't know."

"Call on your home teachers. They'll be glad to give her a blessing."

"Home teachers?"

"Oh, you probably haven't been assigned any yet."

"No. We've only been here a few days."

"We'll get that taken care of tomorrow. See you then. Church starts at nine."

What kind of blessing? I wondered as I walked home.

CHAPTER THREE

Block Schedule

Sunday morning I stayed in bed as usual, listening to the muted sounds of the household waking up. Sleeping in was the best part of the day, and I didn't want to miss any of it.

Suddenly the bedroom door burst open.

"Get up, sleepyhead, we're going to church!"

I rolled over and opened one eye. "Theodore, what are you doing up? Go back to bed."

"Mom says we have to get dressed. We're going to church."

"Why?"

"I don't know. Just get up." He started waving his arms frantically.

"Is that your imitation of an ostrich who can't find a hole to stick his head in?" I rolled over and pretended to go back to sleep.

"Very funny," he said. Theodore started rummaging through his suitcase. "Close your eyes," he demanded when he finally found what he was looking for.

I ignored him. I was supposed to be asleep.

After he left I felt myself peacefully drifting back into unconsciousness. Darwin reached for my hand and we were dancing at the senior prom. I felt his arms around me. We continued to swirl and float upward. The music was soft and distant. I snuggled deeper into my pillow.

"Julie."

"Yes," I whispered.

"Time to get up."

Darwin vanished.

I rolled toward the sound. My father stood in the open doorway. "I'm asleep," I mumbled.

"Not anymore. We're leaving in half an hour. You better get cracking."

"Do I have to?"

"You came out here to be with your mother. It will make her happy."

After he left, I tried to conjure up dreams of Darwin again, but the blissfulness of sleep had vaporized at the mention of my mother. I got dressed instead.

Under duress I walked dutifully up the chapel steps, a scowl tugging at my mouth. Church was not part of the plan when I had decided to come out to Utah with Mom.

Grandpa was holding the door open. His smile almost split his face in two. My mouth curved upward in spite of myself.

As the meeting in the chapel ended I glanced at my watch. Just a little over an hour had gone by. I waited for the people to stand up so I could make my exit as inconspicuously as possible. To my dismay, everyone remained seated and a new meeting started.

"What's going on?" I whispered to Grandma.

"This is the new block schedule, dear." She patted my hand. "We'll go to class in a few minutes."

Twenty minutes later I was ushered into a room with people more or less my same age. Grandma told me it was the young adult class. I took a seat on the back row.

A man in his mid twenties walked into the room and set a stack of books on the table. His piercing blue eyes and square jaw made his otherwise plain features rather interesting. He cleared his throat and the classroom chatter subsided. "I see some new faces here today. Would those who are new please stand up and introduce themselves."

Luckily a girl two rows ahead of me stood up and then someone on the front row. Assuming he had overlooked me, I sighed in relief.

"We almost forgot the girl in the back," the teacher said.

I hesitated, waiting for someone else to speak up. When heads started turning around, my cheeks reddened. "I'm Julie Edwards," I stammered.

"Will you stand up so we can hear you better?"

With everyone staring at me, that was the last thing I wanted to do.

"Where are you from, Julie?"

"New York," I said loudly. "I'm here visiting my grandparents, the Willises."

"My name is Derrick Van Horn. We're always glad to have visitors. Is there a volunteer for the opening prayer?" Mr. Van Horn asked. The class's attention returned to the front of the room.

I couldn't believe it when a hand went up. Someone actually *wanted* to pray in public.

"Joshua," Mr. Van Horn said.

A tall young man with reddish-brown hair styled in close-cropped curls walked to the front of the room. He pushed his horn-rimmed glasses up on his nose and bowed his head. I watched him, fascinated by his sincerity, until I realized that everyone else had their heads bowed. I looked down at my hands until he finished.

"Who was Enos?" the teacher asked to start the class.

"A prophet of God," the girl sitting next to me said.

"What can we learn from his example?"

Joshua's hand shot up. "The importance that prayer should have in our lives."

"Very good. Open your Book of Mormon to Enos, verse 4."

The girl next to me held her book out for me to see.

"Thanks," I whispered. The title of the book seemed familiar. We might have had one in the bookcase back home, but I wasn't sure. This was the first time I had ever seen it open.

Joshua read: "And my soul hungered; and I kneeled down before my Maker, and I cried unto him in mighty prayer and supplication for mine own soul; and all the day long did I cry unto him; yea, and when the night came I did still raise my voice high that it reached the heavens . . ."

How could anybody pray as long as Enos without running out of things to say? There had to be something phoney about the story.

When class was over, the girl with the Book of Mormon spoke for the first time. "Hi, I'm Cindy Patience. Would you like me to show you where Relief Society is."

"Why?"

"It's the next meeting."

"How many more meetings are there?" I groaned.

"Just one."

"Well, that's a relief."

Cindy laughed. "I feel that way sometimes myself. Come on."

I didn't realize when I got to church that I would be there for three hours. When I finally walked out the front door I felt thoroughly indoctrinated.

Cindy walked me home. She had lived in Provo all her life and was planning to go to BYU in the fall. She was the third of six children and had a brother Theodore's age. She also went to church *every* Sunday. That in itself was amazing.

I liked Sundays for lounging and catching up on homework. My family always went out for dinner Sunday evening in New York. I wondered where we would go today.

"Have you seen the temple yet?" Cindy asked.

"No."

"Would you like to visit the grounds this afternoon?"

I hesitated. What was I getting myself into? Just how much religion could I stand in one day. "I'll have to talk to my parents. I don't know what their plans are."

We stopped in front of my grandparents' house. "If you need anything, just call. I live in the two-story house with the picket fence in the next block. Joshua lives across the street in that Spanish-style one. You're lucky," she said as she left.

Yeah, real lucky, I thought, as I walked toward the house. My mother was dying of cancer. I gave up my friends, my lifestyle, and Juilliard School of Music for what? A peculiar people with an even more peculiar way of life and a bedroom I shared with Theodore.

Sunday afternoon the home teachers came over.

"Julie, this is Brother Peterson and his son, Joshua."

"We've met," I said. It bothered me the way he was always pushing his glasses back on his nose.

"Ah yes, you were the new girl in the back," Joshua beamed.

I was sure the smile was more for his great memory than from any joy at having seen me again.

"Well, this is real nice, Julie. You already have a friend," Grandma said.

I grimaced.

"Will you be going to BYU in the fall, Julie?" Brother Peterson asked.

"Yes, I guess so."

"Joshua has already started summer school. Maybe he can show you around campus. How about it, Josh?"

"I have classes tomorrow," he stammered.

"You can take her when you finish. It would be a nice neighborly thing to do."

"That's all right, I have to go to the hospital with Mom tomorrow."

"We'll be back early in the afternoon," Mom cut in. "I think it would be fun, Julie."

"It would be too much trouble," I objected.

"No trouble at all," Brother Peterson said. "Joshua will be here around three."

By the look on his face, I could tell Joshua was as pleased with the plan as I was.

Why were parents always matchmakers? Joshua was too thin, his hair was too curly, he looked like an owl with those glasses on, and he liked reading scriptures too much. There was not one ounce of Darwin in him.

CHAPTER FOUR

Joshua

Three o'clock rolled around with no sign of Joshua. At 3:05 I announced I was going down to the chapel to practice.

"Give him a few more minutes, dear," Mom said, looking up from the book she was reading. When she looked down again, I slipped out the back door.

Whether or not the chapel doors would be open was uncertain, but I needed to walk in the fresh air. There was precious little of that in New York, and clean air was one thing I wanted to enjoy as long as I could.

I had just started playing the theme song from *Chariots of Fire* when the rear door banged open. A red-faced Joshua came puffing up the isle. He sat down on the front row.

"Sorry I'm late," he said when I finished.

I wished he had been later. I guess the thought showed on my face.

"If you're busy, we can go another time. I don't mind." He stood up and started back down the aisle.

His indifference convinced me. "Let's go." I gathered my music and followed him through the doorway and down the sidewalk.

"Do you always walk this fast?"

He stopped abruptly.

"I feel like a squaw walking ten feet behind you." I meant it as a joke, but he didn't laugh.

14

We walked side by side for the next block.

"Do you play the piano?" he finally asked.

"No," I said with sarcasm.

"Oh, sorry. Stupid question."

"What classes are you taking in school?" I asked half a block later.

"The usual."

"Which are?"

"Chemistry, physics, anatomy, biology, all the basic stuff."

"That's a pretty heavy load for one semester. What are you planning to be, a doctor?"

"Yeah."

"What kind?"

"I haven't decided yet."

I looked at his profile. His tight curls were more relaxed today, almost fly away, and his hair picked up light from the sun. Would I trust him with my life? Someone with freckles? When he looked at me I looked away.

"What were you thinking just now?"

"Nothing."

"Come on, I know it was about me being a doctor."

"Why would I think anything about that?"

"You don't think I look the part, right?"

"I didn't say that."

"Tell me the truth."

"Okay. The truth is that I have never seen a doctor with freckles."

"I try to stay out of the sun."

"Have you tried sunblock?"

"Thanks a lot. My freckles are really bad, aren't they?"

"Freckles go with red hair."

"Oh, gee! Now my hair is red." He pulled on some of it in frustration.

"Look, your hair is fine. Your freckles are fine." I glanced across the street. We were passing my grandparent's house. "Are we going to walk all the way to BYU?"

"No, we're going to ride."

The ride turned out to be pedal power. He rode his ten speed and I rode his sister's. It was a long way by bike to the lower end of campus.

The last hill was more like a walkway, but it was too steep to pedal up, especially in the wrong gear. I jumped off before I fell off. I hoped I could find a better way to get to school than this. If I was this tired, my concentration would be shot.

"Hey, Joshua," I panted.

"I'll wait for you at the top," he yelled over his shoulder, still pedaling.

"Thanks a lot," I muttered as he left me behind.

I walked slowly, breathing deeply. The low-hanging trees shaded the walkway. Flowers grew at intervals in splashes of color.

Parts of Central Park in New York were like this. A path wide enough for walkers meandered through the groves of trees and grassy areas. The only thing that was missing was the lake and the sight of skyscrapers through the foliage. Slowly the ground leveled out and some buildings became visible through the trees.

"Ready?" a voice came from behind me.

I dropped the bike, automatically spinning around in my Judo self-defense position. At the sight of Joshua, I relaxed my stance.

"What did I do to deserve that?" Joshua asked.

"Where I come from a girl can never be too careful. You're lucky I don't have my purse." I winked at him. "That's where I keep my Mace." We pedaled side by side toward the buildings.

"Is New York really that bad?" Joshua asked.

He was so naive. "Some places are worse than others. That walkway back there reminds me of Central Park."

Joshua looked over his shoulder. "I thought New York was full of skyscrapers."

"It is, but it has its garden spots too. Take Trump Towers for example."

"You've been there?"

"I lived there for two years."

"What's it like?"

"The lobby is a miniature shopping mall with a four-story indoor waterfall. There are little shops and places to eat, mirrors and green plants. It's spacious with lots of windows. Everything that isn't glass is either brass or pink marble. My favorite place is the outside garden on the fourth flour. Not many people go there, especially in the winter, but it always gave me a place to get away from the crowd."

"Well, here we are." Joshua stopped his bike. "This is the Kimball Building. As you can see, it has over twelve floors. It's the tallest building on campus." He frowned. "You're not impressed. Moving on . . . " He started pedaling toward a low building. "This is the library. We can go inside if you want. Of course, you've seen books before."

He picked up speed and headed toward the end of the building. I pedaled faster to keep up with him. We rounded the corner and started down the side of a large rectangular grassy area.

"Over there," he pointed to his left, "is the Jesse Knight Building. On the right is the Fine Arts and straight ahead is the Administration Building. The neat thing about the Administration Building is that it is in the shape of an X."

"Can we slow down?"

"Oh, sure." His bike ground to a sudden halt. I turned sharply to keep from running into him.

"Is there any place to get a drink? I'm dying of thirst."

"We could try the cafeteria."

After locking our bikes, we went inside. There were still students scattered about at the tables. Some were conversing, while others sat with their books open, nibbling while they studied. Joshua ordered a cone and I got a Diet Sprite. I followed him to the cashier.

His color deepened as he rummaged through his pockets. When his cheeks matched his hair, I casually pulled out a dollar and paid for both of us.

"Thanks," he muttered after we sat down. "My pocket has a hole in it." He pulled the lining out and fingered the frayed edges.

"Don't worry about it."

His freckles gradually became more prominent as his color faded.

"So what are you going to major in?" he asked, licking his cone.

"Music."

"That's nice. Are you going to be a music teacher?"

"I hope not."

"Then why would you major in music?" He licked his cone again and some of it stayed on his chin.

"To become a musician." I handed him my napkin. He missed the spot so I wiped it off for him.

"Wouldn't it be better to go to a school that specializes in music? Isn't there one back east somewhere?"

"You mean the Juilliard School of Music."

"That's the one."

"Juilliard is definitely a better school for musicians . . ."

"Instead you chose BYU. Well, that's what a lot of Mormons do."

I took a sip of my drink. "I'm not a Mormon."

"What?"

"I said, I'm not a Mormon."

"But your parents are. Aren't they?"

Julie shrugged. "They don't practice their religion."

"They were in church Sunday."

"That was the first time in years. I still don't know what got into them."

The ice cream in Joshua's cone started to run down his hand.

"You're getting sticky."

"Oh." He wiped it off. "So why ARE you going to BYU?"

"It was just one of the universities I applied to because it was near my grandparents' home, and I was accepted."

"Did you apply at Juilliard and get turned down?"

I felt the pain as strong as I had that last day in New York. "You're so nosey," I lashed out at him. "Can't you mind your own business?"

"I guess rejection is hard for everyone."

That hurt almost as bad. "I wasn't rejected," I said through clenched teeth.

"Then what are you doing here?"

"Please don't tell my parents. They don't know."

"Why?"

"You ask a lot of questions." I stood up and threw my cup into the nearest garbage can. Joshua followed.

"I'm sorry." He put his hand lightly on my shoulder.

I shrugged it off.

"I always ask too many questions. I'm always putting my foot in my mouth."

I stopped to look at him. His hazel eyes were soft and appealing. "It's all right. I can handle it." I walked a few more feet before hot tears clouded my vision. Pushing on the nearest door I stepped quickly outside. Hearing him behind me, I made a futile wipe at my eyes.

"Can we go home now?" I asked without looking back.

"If you want."

I stayed in the lead until we reached our bikes. It was the sniffling that gave me away.

"Look, Julie, I'm really sorry. I've never made a girl cry before, except maybe my sisters."

"It's not you," I said, brushing away the last of my tears. "It's me."

We rode home in silence.

CHAPTER FIVE

Princess to Pauper

On Thursday Darwin called. I had just washed my hair and was brushing out the snarls.

"Hi, babe. I miss you." His deep voice was loaded with charm.

"I miss you, too."

Theodore chose that moment to walk by. "Mush," he said loud enough for Darwin to hear. I gave him a look that would have withered his cartoon heroes to pencil dots.

"What's going on in New York?" I asked Darwin after Theodore left the room.

"Oh, the usual. Dad keeps me pretty busy working in his office."

"Do you like it?"

"I haven't decided yet."

"What are Francine and Dave doing?"

"They broke up."

"Oh, that's too bad."

"Yeah, I know. I took Francine out to lunch to console her."

"You what?"

"Hey, don't get on your high horse. I would have taken you, too, if you'd been here. It's pretty hard having my girl three thousand miles away."

"It must be," I mumbled. Even though Francine had been my best friend, I didn't trust her where Darwin was concerned.

20

"Hey, what's it like living in Timbuktu, anyway?"

"They do have paved roads here, Darwin."

"Have you got any country bumpkins chasing you yet?"

"No."

"That's good. I want you all to myself." He laughed his deep rumble. We talked for a good half hour, and it seemed as though I'd never left New York.

"Listen, Darwin," I finally said, "I've got to get my hair brushed out before it's completely dry."

After I hung up, I envisioned Darwin and Francine sitting at a candle-lit table for two overlooking the lights of the city. Depression set in. I snapped at Theodore and chased him out of the bedroom. As I brushed my hair, I could hear him whining to Mother through the closed door. Why did he always have to be such a tattletale? And why was Darwin dating Francine? I pulled savagely at a snarl until my eyes watered.

A knock on the door renewed my anger. "Go away, pest," I snarled.

The door opened quietly and Mom stuck her head in. "Mind if I come in?"

My lack of response was interpreted as yes.

"Who was on the phone, Julie?"

"Didn't Theodore tell you?" I spat out.

"He only said that you yelled at him and threatened to hit him."

"I didn't hit him. The little liar." I laid the brush down, opened the nearest drawer, and stared at the contents.

"Julie, that tone of voice isn't like you. What's bothering you?"

"Everything!" I turned around. "Mom, I hate Utah, I hate going to church, and I hate sharing a room with Theodore. When are we going to move into a house of our own?"

"We're working on it. We just have to find the right one."

"Everything we saw yesterday I wouldn't let my dog live in."

Mom laughed. "You don't have a dog."

"We couldn't fit my piano in half the living rooms we saw."

"It may have to have a room all its own."

"Will we be able to live in something as nice as our apartment in Trump Towers?"

Mom shook her head. "Probably not. Most of the money from our savings has got to go into the business here. On top of that, we have to come up with the cost of housing and medical bills."

"Doesn't the insurance cover the medical expenses?"

"Not all of them. We have to be conservative. Your father's not sure what his income will be here."

I felt like a princess suddenly turned into a pauper.

"Mom, what are your chances of beating this thing?"

"What thing?"

"Your sickness." I could not bring myself to say the word *cancer.*

"As good as anyone's."

"But what did the doctor tell you?"

"He said I had a good chance."

"But what percentage?"

"Percentage?"

"Doctors always give percentages in the movies."

"This is real life, Julie. Things aren't as clear cut. The doctor said we caught it early—not as early as he would have liked, but early enough to give me a good chance. I would like to plan on spending many more years with you and your dad."

"But why did we have to move to Utah?" I complained.

Mother sat on the edge of the bed, staring at her reflection in the mirror. After a while she answered softly.

"Because I needed strength."

"But you've always been strong."

"Not with the kind of strength I need now. You see, when I was your age . . ."

Here it comes again, I thought.

"I was very active in the Church. I attended everything from firesides to seminary. I used to be a lot like Cindy, that girl you met at church last week."

"What!" That was the first time I'd ever heard that. "You told me you were the black sheep of the family and proud of it."

"I lied."

"Why?" I asked, confused.

"Because it was easier. When I was a few years older than you are now, I met your father. I had already graduated from BYU and I was working for a small firm in Salt Lake. Your dad transferred out here from Massachusetts on a temporary assignment from the home office. He was an energetic, hard worker and had a head for business. There were lots of things I liked about him. He wasn't a member of the Church, though. I think he joined to please me. When his assignment ended he asked me to marry him. Since he had only been a member a few weeks, we were married civilly and left for Massachusetts the next day.

We planned on a temple marriage, but somehow, with his work schedule and travel, he was never around. On the rare occasions when he was, he was always too busy to attend more than one meeting on Sunday. That quickly changed to hit and miss as we both began attending Sunday business luncheons. Eventually, we had more in common with your dad's business associates than we did with the members of our ward. When he was transferred to New York, we didn't bother requesting our membership records. We were convinced that if you children had the best of material things, you would be well-endowed for life." Mom pulled me down on the bed beside her and put her arm me. "I'm sorry, Julie, but I can see now what a false notion that really was."

"So why are you telling me all this now?"

"Because I might not be able to later."

It had been years since I had hugged my mother, but I did it then. When she left, I cried into my pillow.

That night I decided to pray. I waited until I was sure Theodore was asleep. I didn't bother getting out of bed, but I did I cross my arms like the Mormons did in church. "God," I said, staring at the light fixture in the semidarkness, "I need your help. My mother is . . . (even around God I couldn't use the word *dying*) . . . sick. Please bless her to get well." I repeated the plea over and over again until I drifted into a light, troubled sleep.

CHAPTER SIX

The Seed

The next Sunday in sacrament meeting, I sat next to my mother. A goofy smile was on her face as she listened to the speaker. I couldn't believe she was so captivated.

Disgusted, I took out my nail file. First I sharpened my nails to points and then gradually rounded them off. Next week I would bring my polish.

Theodore sat on the other side of me enthralled as I filed. "It's the macho thing to do these days," I whispered. When I picked up his hand and started filing, he didn't even complain. He was fascinated by the little crumbs of fingernail that were collecting in my lap. When I finished his hand, he brushed wildly at my dress and sent them flying onto the floor. Some caught in the long hair of the girl in front of us.

"Thanks a lot," I hissed.

"Shhhhhh," Mom said.

Theodore smiled cherublike and held out his other hand.

By the time I got to the Young Adult class, there was nothing left to do but listen.

Derrick Van Horn held up a tiny black object. "Even though something is small, it can work mighty miracles. This little thing can create something one thousand times it weight."

"What is it?" a girl asked.

He set a jar of them on the table. The front row leaned forward.

"Watermelon seeds," Joshua said.

A class on gardening, I thought with renewed interest.

"What does this seed represent?" Mr. Van Horn asked.

Joshua's hand shot up. "It represents the word of God."

A watermelon seed? Come on.

"That's right. Turn in your Book of Mormon to Alma 32:28. Cindy, you read first and then pass your book to Julie."

I looked up in surprise. He remembered my name.

"Now, we will compare the word unto a seed," Cindy began.

Now, if ye give place, that a seed may be planted in your heart, behold, if it be a true seed, or a good seed, if ye do not cast it out by your unbelief, that ye will resist the Spirit of the Lord, behold, it will begin to swell within your breasts; and when you feel these swelling motions, ye will begin to say within yourselves—It must needs be that this is a good seed, or that the word is good, for it beginneth to enlarge my soul; yea, it beginneth to enlighten my understanding, yea, it beginneth to be delicious to me.

Brother Van Horn, as everyone else called him, put a paper cup filled with dirt on the table, then he pushed the watermelon seed deep into the soil. "What do we need to make our seed grow?"

"Water," Cindy volunteered.

"Faith," Joshua countered.

Whoever heard of watering a garden with faith? That was crazy.

The teacher pulled an old-fashioned watering can with a long spout out of a paper sack. FAITH was written on the side of the can. "You're both right," he said.

When he watered the seed, the nozzle sprayed wide. "I should have practiced this at home," Brother Van Horn apologized.

After he sent Joshua for some paper towels from the bathroom, he said: "When I was on my mission to Japan, I taught Brother Nakagama. After he heard the word of God, he began watering it with his faith . . . "

At the end of class Brother Van Horn asked me to wait. I hoped he wasn't mad I had laughed when he watered the table.

"Do you have a Book of Mormon with you?" he asked.

"No."

"Would you like to borrow mine?"

"Thank you, but that's not necessary."

"If you don't have one, you won't be able to read next week's assignment."

"Well, ahhh."

"I insist, take mine."

"But . . ."

"Don't worry," he said. "I've got another one at home."

Cindy walked me home from church. Her short blond hair whisked about her face as a gusty breeze assaulted us.

"You're lucky you have long hair," she said. "It's easy to tie back. I wish my hair would grow as long as yours."

I smiled. Although I had thought about cutting it many times, the most I had allowed to be taken off was a couple of inches. "Don't cut it. Let it grow," I advised.

"It wouldn't make any difference. It doesn't grow past my shoulders. See this?" she said, pulling a strand of her hair forward and staring at it cross-eyed. "Look at the difference between yours and mine." She reached for my braid and held the end close to the strand in her hand. "My hair is too thin and curly."

"But your short hair is pretty," I said.

"Yeah, I know. I should just be thankful for what I have instead of envious of what I don't." She sighed. "So how do you like Provo?"

If I answered truthfully, I would hurt her feelings. Instead I shrugged. "How long has Derrick Van Horn been home from Japan?"

"He's been back about four years, long enough to get married and have a baby. He's working on his master's degree at the Y."

"The Y?"

"BYU." She looked at me incredulously. "You MUST be from back East."

"I'll take that as a compliment," I said. "Was Mr. Van Horn on a mission with his parents in Japan?"

Cindy looked at me. "Brother Van Horn went by himself when he was nineteen like everyone else."

"What do you mean by 'everyone else'?"

"All the young men in the ward go when they turn nineteen. My older brother, Benjamin, is on a mission in Panama right now."

"What is he? Some kind of Peace Corps type?"

Cindy laughed. "Sometimes you don't even sound like you're a Mormon."

"I'm not."

She sobered immediately. "You're not? Then why do you go to church?"

"To please my mother."

"Oh."

We walked in silence the rest of the way. When we came to my grandparents' house, I crossed the street and started up the walk. At the top of the steps, I threw the watermelon seeds I'd been given in class in the flower bed. The front door banged closed behind me. I didn't realize at the time that they had fallen in the rich soil of a freshly raked and watered garden.

CHAPTER SEVEN

Punch and Cookies

On Saturday night, Cindy and Joshua escorted me to my first Young Adult party. It was held at the stake center. The "steak" part had influenced my acceptance.

Joshua drove us in his father's pickup truck. He and Cindy told elementary school jokes on the way.

"What's big and red and eats rocks?" Joshua asked.

"A big red rock eater," Cindy said.

I sighed and stared out the window. Joshua would never make it driving taxi in New York City.

When we pulled into the parking lot of a building very similar to the church my grandparents attended I assumed that we were taking a short cut. My assumption was wrong.

"Why did the Mormon cross the road?" Joshua asked.

"To get to the other side," Cindy said.

"No, to get to the stake center."

"Where's the steak center?" I asked.

"This is it," Cindy said.

I sighed again. I should have expected a trick like this.

Joshua jumped out of the truck and walked around to my side. Opening the door, he extended his hand. After jumping down, I looked back at Cindy. She radiated when Joshua took her hand.

Cindy was tall and slim. Her height was very close to Joshua's. The top of my head normally would have come to his shoulder, but I wore three-inch heels. I had a feeling I would regret it later. Most of the other young people we saw were dressed as casually as Cindy and Joshua in jeans and T-shirts.

The first game we played was a relay. The man in charge divided us into groups by our last names. We formed eight lines. Cindy stood next to Joshua. From the look of the two guys on either side of me, I would have liked a last name that started with "P" too. I imagined the names of the two teammates I got stuck between to be Goat and Fats.

The man gave each of us a toothpick. Goat began picking his teeth with it. When he flipped something out on the floor, I shuddered. Backing away, I bumped into Fats. He introduced himself as Freddy, nonchalantly scratching his rotund middle.

"Are you new in town?" Freddy asked.

"Yes." I didn't add "unfortunately."

"Which ward are you in?"

"I'm staying with my grandparents, the Willises."

"Which ward is that?"

I shrugged. "It's the same one as that guy over there with red hair." I pointed to Joshua.

"Oh."

By this time, the people at the front of the lines had been given a package of Lifesavers. A whistle sounded and the first one in each line ripped open his package. To my horror they started passing them down the lines on the toothpicks held between the participants' teeth. From Fats to ME to Goat, I thought. No way.

"I've got a stomach cramp," I said doubling over. "I need to sit down."

Fats helped me to a chair against the wall, getting back just in time to catch a Lifesaver and pass it on to Goat. Their seriousness was amazing.

When a newcomer took my place on the team, I wandered out to look for the kitchen. I still harbored a slim hope of eating steak. No such luck. The kitchen was filled with tray upon tray of homemade cookies. I should have eaten the tuna casserole at Grandma's house.

Pushing open the rest room door, I came face to face with myself in the mirror. My big brown eyes and dark eyebrows gave my face a well sculptured appearance. When I stared long enough at my reflection, I saw the porcelain doll my Grandma Edwards kept on the dresser in her bedroom. She always told me the doll reminded her of me. Maybe I did on the outside, but that was as far as it went. I wasn't delicate or breakable like her porcelain doll.

Sometimes I felt like poking fun at the world. Darwin described me as complex—a mystery woman worth knowing. I liked that. But, I thought as I stared at my reflection, who was I? And what was I doing mixed up with a bunch of Mormons?

I took my brush out of my purse and started counting strokes. I liked my hair's shiny fullness after a hundred brushes. When I reached sixty-seven, the door swung open.

"Oh, there you are," Cindy said. "We were worried about you."

I followed her back to the cultural hall for punch and cookies. As I munched, I thought about my friends in New York. A party to them was dim lights, loud rock music, drinking, and smoking pot. All four of these elements were missing tonight. I wondered what they would think of this party.

Biting into a chocolate-chip cookie, I caught sight of Fats. He munched oblivious to the activity around him. His cheeks bulged and his hands, full of cookies, were waiting to cram more in.

The man in charge announced another game. I set my empty cup on the table and started for the bathroom. Joshua grabbed my arm before I had gone ten feet and pulled me toward the circle of chairs in the center of the floor.

"I'm really not up to this."

"How can you be sure, if you don't try?"

Joshua sat on one side of me and Fats on the other. He stuffed the remaining cookies in his shirt pocket and wiped his hands on his pant legs.

The object of the game was for the person in the center to get a seat from someone in the circle. He did this by naming similar articles of clothing worn by those seated or by saying an eye or hair color. Those who fell into the selected category had to jump up and change seats. The person in the middle tried to take their place.

Fats had it in for me. After several unsuccessful attempts at getting a seat, he walked to my side of the circle. "All those with black hair," he said.

Even though I jumped up quickly, with high heels on I could only take small steps. I headed for the nearest vacant seat, but Goat leaped across the circle and got there a split-second before I did. To my chagrin, I landed in his lap. By the time I apologized and stood up, all the seats were taken. Fats smiled broadly from my recently vacated chair.

"Everyone with blue eyes," I said.

All the blue eyes whirled past me in a blur. I was walking on stilts. My fastest wasn't good enough.

"How about green shirts?" I said hopefully. Unfortunately, all three of them were seated close together. As I looked around the sea of faces, one stood out from the rest. It was Joshua's. His teasing grin was unnerving. I casually moved closer. I was going to get his chair.

"All those wearing jeans," I said. Half the group stood up and I slid easily into his seat.

The respite didn't last long. Almost every time something was mentioned that I was wearing, I ended up in the middle. The only one who was "it" more often than I was Fats, and he picked on me. By the time I'd been up ten times, Joshua's smile had grown to the size of a Jack o'lantern's. I decided to fix him once and for all. "Everyone with freckles," I announced.

He hesitated. I covered the short distance between us and stood waiting. Reluctantly he gave up his seat and stalked to the center. When he looked at me I saw I had successfully changed his grin to a scowl. I wasn't sure I liked it better.

"All those with high heels," Joshua said.

There were two of us. The other girl was on the far side of the circle. We both started for each other's chair. Joshua moved slowly, arriving just before I did. His teasing grin was back. I decided not to try freckles again.

On the way home, Joshua dropped Cindy off first. He pulled into his driveway and then opened the door for me. He kept hold of my hand as we walked across the street to Grandma's house.

"How did you like the party?" he asked.

"Do you want the truth?"

He laughed. "I don't know."

"I haven't been to a party like that since I was in sixth grade."

"It was that bad?"

"No, it was that *good*." I smiled at him, but I couldn't see his eyes behind his horn-rimmed glassed. His freckles didn't show up in the dark.

"They're gone," I said.

"What?"

"Your freckles."

We walked back to the truck so he could look in the side mirror. Sitting down on the curb, I took off my shoes and wiggled my toes.

"Boy, that feels good."

Joshua joined me. "Why do you wear them?"

"Wear what?"

"High heels?"

"Because I'm short. I get tired of looking up. Don't you like girls in high heels?" I teased.

"I can take them or leave them."

"You're sure different from the other guys I know."

"Is that good or bad?"

Before I had a chance to answer he grabbed my hand and dragged me barefoot across the street.

Pulling off his tennis shoes, he tied the laces together, stuffed his socks inside and hung them around his neck. Then he rolled up his pants and waded into a small stream of water running down the gutter.

"Come on," he said, taking a few steps.

I hesitated. "Won't we get a disease or something?"

"In Provo? I used to do this all the time when I was a kid."

Gingerly I poked a toe into the cold water and then submersed my entire foot. Leaving my shoes on the sidewalk, I followed the overgrown kid to the end of the block.

"How do you like it?"

"It's sort of fun, considering."

"Considering what?"

"Considering it's dark and no one can see what I'm doing."

We turned around and headed back. I was in the lead. "Now I know why you picked on me at the party," I said.

"I didn't pick on you," Joshua countered.

I felt water hit the back of my legs. Ignoring it, I walked faster.

When water hit me again, I spun around and kicked some back at Joshua. "Cut it out!"

"Sorry." He looked sheepishly at his feet.

A minute later I felt a third spray of water.

"You're making me mad," I hissed without turning around. Suddenly water was pouring over the top of my head. Spinning around, I got the rest in my face.

"You're using your shoes to dump water on me!"

"They're washable."

"Give me those!" Grabbing his shoes by the laces, I filled them both and threw a spray of water at him.

He retreated too fast and slipped, landing in the gutter.

"How does it feel?" I taunted.

"Do you really want to know?"

Dripping wet, he chased me as I ran up the sidewalk to my grandparents' house. I made the mistake of stopping for my shoes and he caught me.

Screaming, I tried to wiggle out of his grasp as he dragged me back toward the gutter.

The front door opened and Dad stepped out on the porch. "Is that you, Julie?"

Joshua dropped me like a hot poker. Realizing his mistake, he offered me his hand. I got up without his help.

"Who's that with you, Julie?"

"It's Joshua Peterson, Dad," I said, brushing my hair out of my face.

"Oh yes, the home teacher. Isn't it a little late to be visiting?"

"Yes sir. I mean, no sir. I was just bringing Julie home from the Young Adult party."

We walked toward the light.

"And you slipped in the gutter?" Dad asked.

Joshua looked at me. "Something like that."

Dad grunted. "Julie, you've got a call from New York," he said.

I hurried up the steps without looking back.

"It's the third time he's called this evening," Dad said before the door closed.

CHAPTER EIGHT

The Apricot Tree

A re you baptized, yet?"

"Who is this?" I asked. My wet hair dripped onto the phone.

"Have you forgotten me so soon, Julie?"

"Darwin!" I said, brushing the water off.

"What's so funny?" he asked.

"It's nothing." I giggled again as more drops fell.

"Tell me what's going on."

I looked around the room to make sure I was alone, then I whispered, "You just asked me if I was baptized and I'm standing here dripping wet."

"Ha, you did it! I told you they would get you. A bet is a bet and I win."

His enthusiasm irked me. "Is that all you care about, winning a stupid bet?" I hissed. "I'm not baptized, Darwin. I'll never be."

"Then why are you dripping wet? Is it raining or something?"

I thought about Joshua falling into the gutter and then chasing me like a ten-year-old. His about-face when Dad walked out on the porch had been comical. Did Darwin want to hear about Joshua?

"It's raining," I finally said. Somewhere in the world, I thought.

"I've been doing a little research you might be interested in before you take the plunge," Darwin said chuckling. "Did you know that Mormons can have up to twenty-seven wives?"

"Really?" I didn't remember meeting any extra wives at church, but then I'd only been twice.

"It's true. One of their prophets had twenty seven. He's the one with the same last name as that university you're going to attend."

"Brigham Young?"

"That's the one."

"Look, Darwin. I know my Uncle Bill's only married to one wife, Aunt Jean. Are you sure?"

"Polygamy is alive and well in Utah."

"How do you know that?"

"I found a pamphlet in the library."

His smugness bothered me. "Isn't polygamy against the law?" I asked. The Mormons were simple, unsophisticated maybe, but not law breakers.

"Who knows what the backward states are getting away with."

"Darwin," I said a little too sharply, "you've never been out West. You don't know what you're talking about."

"I told my father I wanted to get to know the U.S. better this summer. I suggested I could start by flying out to Utah."

"So when are you coming?" My heart skipped a beat.

"I'm not. They insisted I go with them to France. It's sort of like the last family vacation together before I start college. It means a lot to them."

"You're going to Paris." Depression struck harder because it replaced the excitement of a moment ago.

"Only for a couple of days. Most of our time will be spent on the Riviera."

"How long?"

"Dad can only take off two weeks. The rest of us may stay longer. We're leaving tomorrow so I had to call you tonight."

Everything else he said was a blur. Darwin was leaving for what seemed like forever. While he swam along the Riviera, I would be stuck in Hicksville wading in the gutter.

Sunday I woke with the sniffles. It was my excuse to stay home from church. After the others had gone, I sat in the front room flipping through an old copy of *Seventeen* magazine, thinking about Mom. At breakfast she had only nibbled on her toast. When she was ready to leave, she had given me a lingering hug and a peck on the forehead. Her thin smile didn't hide the paleness in her cheeks. What if Mom died in church? I closed the magazine and threw it on the coffee table. It slid off and landed on the floor. I wished she had insisted I go with her. I didn't worry as much when I was with her.

When Mom came home from church, she rested while Grandma and I fixed lunch. By four o'clock, Mom was asleep on the couch. Grandpa was off on some kind of church errand, and I was sure the day couldn't get any bluer.

Grandma, Dad, Theodore, and I sat around the kitchen table playing Scrabble. The popcorn had been eaten down to the old maids and I had a collection of consonants that even Shakespeare couldn't spell with. Even Theodore had racked up more points than I had.

When the doorbell rang, I jumped up to answer it. The conspiring duo, Cindy and Joshua, stood on the front porch.

"We came by to see how you're feeling," Cindy said.

"I felt a cold coming on this morning," I explained.

Joshua stood a little behind Cindy with his arms folded. His self-righteous stance bothered me.

"I feel fine now," I added, glaring at him.

"We're glad you're feeling better," Cindy said.

"I guess I got a little too wet last night," I said, baiting Joshua. A smile flickered on his lips.

"Wet?" Cindy asked.

"It started to rain a little after we dropped you off," Joshua cut in.

Somewhere in the world, I thought. Satisfied by his uneasiness, I stepped out on the porch. "My mother's asleep on the couch."

"Should we come back another time?" Cindy asked.

Suddenly the door swung open behind me and Theodore stuck his head out. "It's your turn, Julie. Hurry up. We're all waiting."

"Count me out," I said. "I've got friends over." The only reason Theodore looked disappointed was because he liked gloating about his higher scores. If I didn't finish the game, I wouldn't loose.

"But Julie," he whined.

"Don't wake Mom," I warned.

"Are you in the middle of something?" Joshua asked.

"Not anymore." I walked past him down the steps. "Want an apricot?"

They followed me around back. I liked my grandparents' yard from the first time I saw it. Grapevines were growing on arched trellises along the side of the house. In another week or two the bunches of tiny green fruit would be a burden even for the sturdy vines. Grandpa had nurtured them for years. Now they were so thick they formed a leafy tunnel leading around back. Joshua had to duck under the last of the vines at the back of the house.

Half of the area in the backyard was a garden with neat rows of beans, tomatoes, and corn. Early every morning, except Sunday, I heard the scraping sounds of Grandpa's hoe. There were no weeds in his garden.

In the middle of the backyard was an oak tree. It was surrounded by a neatly hedged section of grass. Hanging from one of its branches was an old tire swing. I gave the tire a twirl as I walked past, making a beeline for the gnarled apricot tree in the far corner. It had been growing so long it was almost as high as the oak.

"There are only a few ripe ones," I said, looking up.

Without hesitating Joshua pulled himself onto a lower branch of the tree. "How's this?" he asked reaching for a semi-orange apricot.

"The one above it is a little riper," Cindy said.

Joshua climbed higher. After dropping several to us, he started down.

"When did you learn to climb trees?" I asked.

"When I was about five."

"Is it easy?"

"Give me your hand."

It looked easy enough. I handed my apricots to Cindy. "I've never done this before."

"Not even as a kid?" she asked.

Joshua pulled me up to his branch. I was too busy holding on to answer. He eased the death grip I had on his hand around the trunk of the tree. Grabbing too small of a branch with my other hand, I snapped it off swinging backwards into him.

"You ARE an amateur," he laughed.

37

"And I suppose you're a professional," I challenged.

"Watch." He steadily climbed upward to about ten feet above my head.

"Is he always such a smart aleck?" I asked Cindy. Reaching up I started to follow him.

"Only grab the biggest branches," Cindy advised. "Make sure your footing is solid."

Five minutes later, I had hold of the same branch Joshua did. Sweat trickled into my eyes and I rubbed my face on my sleeve. It was hotter than I thought.

"Not bad," I said, pleased with myself.

"Not bad for a beginner," he teased.

I ignored him and looked around. The perspective of everything in the garden was different twenty feet up. I was at the same height as the knot holding the swing in the oak tree. It had seemed so high before. I picked an apricot and ate it. The fruit was definitely better higher up in the tree. I picked another one and stuck it in my shirt pocket. I might try climbing up here again sometime.

"Are you guys going to stay up there all day?" Cindy asked.

I looked down and then wished I hadn't. Cindy was an awfully long ways down. My hands started sweating profusely. "How do we get down?" I whispered to Joshua.

He laughed. I was frightened to death and he laughed.

"It's not funny," I said between clenched teeth. Hanging on tightly with the opposite arm, I wiped first one hand and then the other on my pant legs. The last thing I wanted to do was lose my grip.

It was probably the sweat trickling into my eyes again that finally convinced Joshua I wasn't kidding. He squeezed past me and told me exactly where to place my hand or foot with each move I made. It seemed like an hour before my feet were finally on the ground.

"Shaken, but not stirred," I quoted from *The Spy Who Loved Me*. James Bond was one of Dad's favorite characters.

"Just squashed," Cindy said, staring at my shirt. The ugly stain of apricot juice oozed through my pocket. This would never have happened to the beautiful Russian agent. Carefully I reached inside and pulled out what was left of the apricot.

"Delicious," I said, taking a bite on the good side. After all the trouble to get it, I was determined to eat it. Walking over to the hose, I washed the juice off my shirt. The cold water felt good.

"Hot, Joshua?" I asked, spraying him before he had a chance to answer. "That was for laughing."

CHAPTER NINE

Chemotherapy

Exactly three weeks to the day my mother started her chemo-therapy, she threw up on the way home from the hospital. Grandma was driving and I was sitting next to Mom in the front seat. All I could find was a smashed McDonald's sack. Mom couldn't wait for me to open it. Although the bag missed the first heave, I didn't.

When Mom finished she lay back on the seat moaning, her fore-head creased, her eyes slits. I rolled down the window and breathed deeply. The rush of the wind in my face took the smell away and squelched my own gag impulse. As awful as I felt, Mom felt worse. Then I chuckled. "Why did the chicken cross the road?"

"To get to the other side," Grandma said.

"No. To get out of the way."

"Very funny," Mom groaned.

I told them all the Joshua and Cindy jokes I could remember from the night of the Young Adult party, making a few changes here and there to fit the situation.

"Next time we'll have some plastic bags, Gloria," Grandma cut in. She lead-footed it the rest of the way home.

I helped Mom toward the house while Grandma cleaned up the car. I didn't envy her the job.

"Shall I turn the hose on?" I asked as we walked past the outlet.

"That won't be necessary," Grandma said.

Theodore and Sam, Cindy's little brother, ran around the corner of the house. "NASTY!" Theodore yelled when he saw the car.

They followed us inside. "What's that awful smell?" Theodore asked.

"Guess," I said turning around.

"YUCK!"

"Mom's sick, okay?" I said.

" . . . and so are you," he added. "P-U!" Fanning his nose, he walked quickly back the way he had come, pulling Sam with him.

"Make yourself useful and go help Grandma," I yelled after him.

"Don't worry about Theodore," Mom said. "Just help me into the bathroom and I can do the rest." Her face contorted. "Look what I did to you!"

"It will wash off. Don't worry about it."

I left Mom in the main bathroom and went to use the smaller one in Grandma's bedroom. I didn't think she would mind.

Chemotherapy dealt harshly with its victims, as I was beginning to find out. I had a feeling this was only the tip of the conductor's baton. Mom had months of treatment left to go before . . . before what? She would probably suffer through all the side effects for nothing, and there wasn't anything I could do about it.

Disgusted, I gave up trying to pick the food out of my hair. I needed complete submersion in water to get clean. Climbing into Grandma's shower, I left my soiled clothes in a careful pile on the floor. When I got out, I rinsed them off with the hose in the backyard before throwing them into the washer.

Grandma bought a box of kitchen trash bags and put them in the car. She placed other boxes strategically throughout the house. Grandma prided herself on being prepared.

"Look at this," Mom said, showing me a brush full of hair a few days later. "The doctor said I might lose some hair, but this much is horrifying. Does my hair look thinner in the back?"

I squinted. "No, it looks about the same."

In another week squinting didn't help, especially with Theodore around.

"Wow, what happened to your hair, Mom?" he asked one day at breakfast.

"What's wrong with it?" Mom demanded.

"There's just so much of it missing."

Mom burst into tears and left the room.

"Now see what you've done, you brat," I hissed.

Theodore left, too.

Later as I was washing the dishes and feeling sorry for Mom, I heard someone knocking on a door. Walking to the hallway leading to her bedroom, I overheard Theodore.

"Why don't you get a wig, Mom?" he said. "Then no one can tell."

In the afternoon, that is exactly what she did.

Mom started out wearing her wig only to church on Sunday. After a while, she wore it to the hospital every day. It became so much a part of her that she eventually bought another one to wear while she washed and styled the dirty one.

"I don't have to sit with rollers in my hair anymore," she joked one day. "My hair sits all by itself."

Every few days she would come up with another hair joke. "If I wanted to, I could just drop my hair off at the beauty parlor and go shopping, or I could go swimming and change into dry clothes and dry hair at the same time."

"What am I going to do if the house catches on fire and I can't find my wig?" she asked one day.

"You could pretend like you were Yul Bryner," Theodore said.

Although Mom laughed, she started wearing a wig to bed.

Sundays were days to be dreaded. Mom slept on the couch after church. It was literally her day of rest from chemotherapy. Dad wandered around aimlessly. Theodore continued to beat me at Scrabble. If I didn't go to church, the day lasted twice as long. Church became a habit.

Bob Roberts, the choir director, stopped me one Sunday as I was leaving the building with Cindy.

"I'm glad I caught you," he said. "Shirley Reynolds, the choir pianist, had her baby early this morning and can't play for choir practice. Could you help us out?"

"Sure she can. She plays beautifully," Cindy volunteered.

I had played a couple of songs for Cindy on her ancient upright piano. This was the thanks I was getting.

"I'm not familiar with the music," I said, hoping to wiggle out of it.

"Frankly, I'm desperate. We're supposed to sing for stake conference in two weeks. If you could just play an introduction and some of the melody, I would be eternally grateful."

"When are the practices?"

"Sunday, immediately after church," Brother Roberts said.

"You mean right now?"

"Yes." He looked apologetic and wistful at the same time.

"I'll stop by your house and tell your folks in case you don't see them," Cindy offered.

I succumbed to pressure. With a friend like Cindy, I was glad I didn't have enemies in Utah.

Following Bob Roberts back inside the chapel, I sat down at the piano and ran quickly through the first song. I actually liked the sentimentality of the music.

At Brother Roberts's cue, I played the introduction. When I got to the first verse, the choir came in so strong, I hit the wrong note.

Playing accompaniment was difficult. I had to watch the music and Brother Roberts at the same time. He added crescendos, ritards, and formatas that weren't written in the music. It took a few times through each piece before I had the hang of his style of conducting.

For the last song, the choir sang "O My Father." The beauty of the music and verse together was more moving than anything I had felt while playing Beethoven or Chopin.

When Brother Roberts dismissed the choir, I gathered up the music to give back to him.

"So, you CAN play the piano!"

I jumped.

It was Joshua.

"What are you doing here?" I asked.

"I sing in the choir."

"You do?"

"I sat right over there for the whole practice."

He sounded perturbed. The piano was turned for a clear view of the choir director, which didn't include a view of all the members. He hadn't been in my line of vision. "Sorry, I was watching the director. Excuse me," I said. "I've got to turn this music in."

I walked over to Bob Roberts. He shied away from the sheets as if they were infested with the bubonic plague.

"You keep them," he said, putting his hands in his pockets. "I don't know how long Shirley will take to recover. You don't mind do you?" he asked.

"She plays great, doesn't she?" Joshua slapped me on the back. I frowned. Who's side was he on anyway? And why was he following me?

"We really need your help next week," Bob Roberts pleaded.

"She doesn't mind at all." Joshua took the music I was trying to get rid of and put it inside his Book of Mormon. "Ready?" he asked.

When we got outside I exploded. "Since when do you make my decisions for me? I'm the one that has to put the work in. I should be able to make up my own mind without you butting in."

"I thought you enjoyed playing for the choir."

I remained silent.

"Look," he finally said, "I was only trying to make it easier for you."

"With friends like you, who needs enemies?" I retorted.

He only smiled and quickened his pace to keep up with me.

CHAPTER TEN

The Blessing

Sunday afternoon Mom was in her usual place, catnapping on the sofa. The rest of us were playing the game Life on the dining room table.

Suddenly Mom stretched and asked, "Who's winning?"

"I am," Theodore said.

I rolled my eyes. "He cheats."

"I do not." Theodore kicked me under the table.

"Dad," I complained.

"We have visitors coming at four. You two better behave your-selves," he said.

"Who's coming?" Theodore asked.

"It's a surprise," I said, pretending to know.

"Tell me," he begged.

"If you know, it will ruin the surprise."

"Julie's right. Wait and see."

My moment of triumph was dampened by my curiosity. Who was coming? When Mom got up to straighten her wig, I followed.

I was still brushing my hair when the doorbell rang. It was the home teachers, Brother Peterson and Joshua. At least their visit would take my mind off losing to Theodore again.

After a while, they started talking about a blessing. Mom had asked for one. I sat back enthralled. Even if it didn't work, it would still be entertaining.

"Is Brother Willis here?" Joshua's dad asked.

Grandma looked at her watch. "He said he'd be back by four."

"We'll have to wait for him, then. I need his help for the blessing."

I watched Dad sitting on the couch holding Mom's hand. It was obvious that he loved her. He was probably tolerating all this blessing ritual just to show her that he cared.

I wondered if they had special robes to put on like I'd seen priests wear in the movies. Brother Peterson was wearing the same suit and tie he had worn to church. I didn't see any bags for extra clothing. How could they pull this thing off without the right attire?

Grandpa had gone over to Stan Johnson's to help him get his car started. He had said something about the ox being in the mire when he left. By the look of his clothes when he walked into the living room, it was obvious he had climbed into the mire with the ox. Grandpa walked right through without stopping. When he finally came back he was wearing a suit and tie.

Brother Peterson asked Mom to sit on a dining room chair, then pulled out a small vial of something and poured some on her wig. I knew she was going to be mad when she found out what he'd done.

Grandpa and Brother Peterson placed their hands on Mom's head and started praying. How could anything so simple work? I was expecting them to cross themselves and perform an elaborate ceremony. This was too simple.

However, when I thought about it, I had never seen a Mormon cross himself. I looked at Joshua with his head bent and arms folded. Next time I got the chance, I would ask him why they didn't.

Brother Peterson stopped praying and Grandpa started. The deep rich sound of his voice echoed sincerity. Closing my eyes, I concentrated on what he was saying.

". . . and by your faithfulness you will be blessed. You will be given the strength to endure. Remember who you are, a daughter of God. He loves you and wants you to be happy . . . Through your faith and the faith of those who love you, you can be made whole and well."

When the blessing ended, Mom was in tears. She shook Brother Peterson's hand and hugged Grandpa. Dad had a wistful expression on his face I didn't understand, and Theodore had actually been reverent during the whole episode. I caught Joshua watching me, and I looked away. I didn't want to give away any secrets about how I was feeling.

Later Grandma sent Theodore and me out to pick grapes for the Petersons. Joshua followed along.

"Do you want them with or without seeds?" I asked.

Joshua reached up and picked several off the vine overhead. Popping them into his mouth he mumbled, "With."

Theodore copied him, except he couldn't reach as high and had to settle for some grapes lower down.

"Are you ready?" Joshua asked. He drew a line in the dirt with his foot. Theodore moved up beside him.

"Count to three, Julie," Theodore commanded.

When I got to three, they spit their seeds out. Even though Theodore leaned across the line, it didn't help. His fell two feet short of Joshua's.

"That's got to be the most revolting thing I've ever seen!" I exclaimed.

"Best two out of three," Theodore said. They took turns counting because I refused to be a part of it.

Picking grapes, I kept my back to them as I filled Grandma's little basket. Theodore was starting to act just like everybody else. It was totally disgusting. When I was almost finished, he gave up.

"You try it, Julie," he said in frustration.

"Theodore, you're crazy if you think I'm going to spit seeds all over the ground."

"Please," he begged. "Do it for the family honor."

"Forget it, Theodore," Joshua said. "She doesn't have the lips for it."

"What?" I turned on him. "What do lips have to do with spitting seeds?"

"Everything."

I picked two grapes from the ones I had collected and chewed them up. Swallowing everything except the seeds, I stepped up to the battle line.

"Ready," I said positioning a seed on the tip of my tongue.

Theodore counted for us.

My first shot almost fell on my toes. Joshua hooted and Theodore groaned. Determinedly I ate another grape. With each try, the seeds landed a little farther out. By the fifth try, Joshua stopped laughing.

Lining up for the seventh time, I glared at him. "This time you eat dirt."

My seed sailed through the air, landing five inches beyond his.

Theodore jumped up and down yelling, "Way to go, Julie!"

"Now, who has the best lips?" I demanded. Picking another bunch of grapes for the basket, I carried it into the house.

CHAPTER ELEVEN

A Forever Family

Monday was set aside for family night. It was Mom's idea. When she got home from the hospital, she lay on the couch reading through an old family night resource book.

Theodore and I were assigned to make a treat. I was willing to settle for Jell-o, but Theodore wanted something he could sink his teeth into. Grandma didn't have any chocolate for brownies, so she sent me to the store. When I got back, she got out a dusty bag of pecans and handed Theodore a hammer. He shelled while I mixed up the batter. We managed to turn a ten-minute job into a two-hour production.

After dinner, we sat in the living room stumbling through the Primary song "Families Can Be Forever." As our voices drifted out of tune, I stopped singing. If only I had my piano, this wouldn't sound so bad, but Ruwanda was sitting in storage with our other furniture, waiting for us to move into a house. To my surprise, Theodore said the opening prayer.

Mom set a picture on the coffee table of a family holding hands. In the background was the Salt Lake Temple.

"Families can be together forever," she said. "What do we need to do to become a forever family?"

"We have to live worthy lives," Grandpa said.

"That's right, if we do what the Lord tells us, if we obey his commandments, we can be together forever."

Theodore raised his hand. "How long is forever?"

"Forever never ends; it goes on even after we die," Grandma answered.

"You mean I have to live with Julie THAT long?"

"Thanks a lot, Theodore. You're no great prize yourself," I said.

Mom pointed to the temple. "In order to be a forever family, we have to be sealed together in one of these."

I thought of all of us cooped up and stuck together forever inside the building Mom was pointing to. No fresh air. No green grass. No new places to go and Theodore constantly at my elbow. It was not a pretty picture.

"What does sealed together mean?" I asked.

"It means that the family bonds we have on earth will never be broken," Grandpa said.

"It means that even though one of us may die," Mom added, "we will still be a family."

The word *die* hit hard. How could she talk so freely about her coming death. I would probably only have a mother another couple of months and then, BINGO. Our family would be broken up. Dad would live a sorry life drowning in his tears. He would probably become an alcoholic. His sorrow would drive him to it. Theodore would become a juvenile delinquent without Mom to guide him, and I would go back to Juilliard and lose myself in my music, playing night and day, only stopping to eat and sleep. I would eventually become a world-renowned pianist, noted for playing only sad melodious music and bringing my audiences to tears at every concert.

The word *baptism* brought me back to the present. Dad was reading a quotation. "To be a forever family," he read, "we have to obey the commandments, which include baptism and sealing in the temple. Parents, you must be married in the temple and have your families sealed to you to be together forever." Dad reread the quote to himself before putting it back on the table.

Mom passed out pieces of a puzzle. "Each of us are like these pieces. We have to work together to see the whole picture and be a family unit."

When we put all our pieces together they formed a picture of a smiling house. Mom taped the picture together and mounted it on a piece of construction paper. At the bottom she printed the words "Forever Family."

The highlight of the evening came after we finished eating our brownies. Casually wiping his hands on a napkin, Dad announced that Saturday we would move into our new house.

Early Tuesday morning Theodore and I walked to the next block for a better look at the house we were moving into. I recognized it immediately from the big red "Sold" printed diagonally across the real estate sign. It was disappointingly similar to the house my grandparents lived in. It had the same porch and the same sloping roof. However, the grass needed cutting and the flower beds were empty. We didn't bother going around back.

Instead we continued up the street to Cindy's house. I wanted to escape from the letdown I felt, and Theodore wanted to play with Sam, Cindy's little brother.

Sam answered the doorbell. He and Theodore ran around back to jump on the trampoline while I waited on the porch for Cindy.

"You picked a good time to visit," she said. "Today is my day off." Cindy had a summer job working at one of the fast-food chains in Provo.

I followed her inside. As we walked through the kitchen she stopped abruptly. "We got a letter from Ben yesterday. Do you want to read it?" When she handed it to me, several photos fell to the floor. I picked them up and gawked at the tall blond. Now *there* was someone who could challenge Darwin's good looks.

"Is this your brother?" I asked.

Cindy leaned over my shoulder. "That's Benjamin, all right."

"He sure is tall."

"He only looks that tall because his companion is so short. He's barely over six feet."

That made him two inches taller than Darwin. Although he wasn't quite as broad shouldered, his handsome features—gorgeous smile, high cheek bones, and penetrating blue eyes—made up for it. I held the picture up to the light from the window. Benjamin's thick stock of blond hair was too short to give him anything but a clean-cut look.

"Cute, isn't he?" Cindy said.

I chuckled and looked at the next picture. Benjamin was standing on the grass in front of a white house.

"That's the church," Cindy said. "Meeting houses are not quite as big in Panama as the ones here."

In the next photo, Benjamin was dressed in white. In fact, everyone in the picture was wearing white. "Who are these people?" I asked.

"They're some people Ben baptized."

I set the photos down. There was that word *baptize* again. It made me uncomfortable.

"Want to see some more family photos?" Cindy asked.

I followed her back to the living room and waited while she pulled out a large album. "This was years ago when Sam was still a baby."

Benjamin, as a boy, looked a lot like Sam did now. "You can tell you are all brothers and sisters," I said. I saw the Patience family in the mountains, at school, on birthdays, and at Disneyland. Benjamin still wore braces when he was at Disneyland. In the last picture taken before his mission, his braces were gone and his smile was dazzling.

"Those braces paid off," I said.

"What?" Cindy asked.

"Benjamin has a nice smile," I blushed.

"Ohh," she said, as if she understood more than she really did.

Before I left she asked me if I could help her out. I nodded, forgetting to ask what it was I would be doing.

"Benjamin needs to get more letters from home. I just don't have enough time to write."

"And you want me to write to him?"

"Only if you want to."

"I don't know what to say."

"Don't worry about it. I'll have him write to you first."

CHAPTER TWELVE

The Duet

On Friday Cindy stopped by on her way to BYU to check on her registration. Since Mom was taking her usual long afternoon nap I decided to go along.

Cindy took the scenic route, pointing out places of interest as she drove. The city park and the supermarket I could hardly call interesting, but on the north side of campus near the temple was a large brick building I'd never seen before.

"That's the MTC," Cindy said. The doors opened and young men wearing white shirts and ties poured out.

"Why are all those students wearing the same thing?" I asked. "You didn't tell me BYU had uniforms."

"Those aren't students," Cindy laughed. "Those are missionaries. MTC is short for Mission Training Center. It's where members of the Church go to be trained as missionaries."

They were Benjamin clones. The replicas even carried black books like Ben had been holding in front of the chapel in Panama.

"How long does the training take to become a missionary?" I asked.

"You should prepare all your life."

"Is that why you go to church so long on Sunday?"

"Something like that. But the actual time you spend in the MTC depends on whether or not you need to learn a foreign language."

"How long was your brother there?" I asked.

"Two months."

"Only two months?"

"It's a crash course. You eat, sleep, and breathe the language."

"And if you don't need a language?"

"Three weeks."

I shrugged. How could anyone learn what they needed to know in three weeks? "So what does your church pay its missionaries?" I asked.

"Nothing. Benjamin is paying for his own mission with a little help from Mom and Dad."

Minimal training and paying your own expenses. The Church of Jesus Christ of Latter-day Saints certainly had a hold over its people. They sent the brainwashed out to brainwash the world. When we finished at the Administration Building Cindy suggested we visit the Wilkinson Center. After touring the building we stopped for a drink at the cafeteria. I thought about Joshua with a hole in his pocket.

Saturday morning a large moving van pulled up in front of our new house. Ten minutes after we started to unload, Joshua and his dad showed up with reinforcements—among them Derrick Van Horn, the Sunday School teacher, and Bob Roberts, the choir director.

I looked down at my faded T-shirt and groaned. I'd worn the one with a rip in the bottom because Dad had said to wear something I could throw away afterwards. Ducking quickly into the bathroom, I tucked the shirt into my jeans. I looked into the mirror and frowned. No makeup. Pinching my cheeks and biting my lips until they reddened, I ran my fingers through my straggly ponytail.

"How's it going?" Joshua asked when I opened the bathroom door.

"I hate moving day," I said, startled.

"That's what home teachers are for."

"What?"

"To help out. Where does this box go?" he asked.

"Theodore" was scribbled on the side of it. "It goes in the room on the right."

I hurried outside, leaving Joshua to find the room by himself. I hadn't expected to see anyone I knew today. Thanks to Dad, I looked like something that needed to be thrown away with the packing paper. Picking up a box, I tried to hide behind it as I carried it into the house. Joshua smiled at me anyway.

Joshua came to my rescue later as I was dragging a big box labeled "dishes" up the front steps.

"Thanks," I muttered.

When we got to the kitchen, Grandma and Mom were washing cupboards. Mom seemed to have more energy than usual. She was actually humming. "Put that box next to those other two," Mom said, a lilt in her voice.

Joshua followed me back outside for another load. "You don't have to help us move in, you know," I said.

He smiled and pushed his horn-rimmed glasses back on his nose. "What would be the point of having home teachers, then?"

We grabbed another big box and carried it toward the house. "I know you're not really our home teachers. We just happened to be at Grandma's house when you came."

"Ok, then—that's what neighbors are for."

"We're not your neighbors anymore. We live a block away."

"Julie, will you stop being so difficult?"

"Me, difficult? I'm just trying to let you off the hook. There's got to be a million other things you'd rather be doing this morning. We're not a charity case," I added and then regretted it.

"I don't mind," Joshua said. "I like helping." He tilted his head toward the other men from the ward hauling boxes. "And so do they."

Dad was giving instructions *con brillo* as he waltzed about the yard trying to be everywhere at once. When the van was nearly empty, I heard Dad say something about a piano.

"Ruwanda!" I exclaimed, setting down the lamp I was carrying and hurrying back to the van.

Joshua picked up the lamp and carried it inside. "Your living room is in a funny place," he said when he came back out.

"What?" I was busy watching the men drag a heavy crate to the door of the moving van.

"You left your lamp on the front lawn."

"I did?"

"What's in that big box?" he asked giving up.

"My piano." Ruwanda was laying flat without legs in a specially built container.

"What happened? Did it fall over?"

"No." I looked at him annoyed. "It's a baby grand."

As the men lifted it out of the truck, I broke out in a cold sweat. Joshua moved in to help them, and I ran up the front steps, swinging the door wide. The crate had to be opened before Ruwanda could fit through the doorway. Even then it was a tight squeeze.

Fortunately, Mr. Peterson was pretty good at putting things together. Joshua went home for their toolbox, then several men held the piano up while Mr. Peterson and I screwed the legs and pedals on.

I suddenly remembered Mom's appointment and ran to the kitchen. She had already gone with Grandma. When I got back to the living room, Joshua was playing a simplified version of "Clair de Lune," a song I had learned years ago.

"That was a nice rendition," I said, "for a beginner."

Joshua grinned. "You have to admit, it's better than nothing."

"Yeah, a little better," I teased. "Do you know any more songs?"

"Sure he does." Mr. Peterson said crawling out from behind the piano.

"Not from memory, Dad."

"After all this work, you've got to play something else, son."

"Let's make 'Clair de Lune' a duet," I offered, sitting down next to Joshua on the piano bench. We played on different octaves of the keyboard. The second time through, I added a countermelody. When we finished, several of the men surrounding the piano applauded.

"Hey, you two sound great together," Derrick Van Horn said. "Have you got an encore?"

"Not me," Joshua said, standing up, "but Julie has."

I played Bach's Minuet Three in G major. Sitting in the box-strewn living room running through my old favorites, I felt a strange sensation of coming home.

At noon, Dad sent Joshua and me out for hamburgers.

"It looks like you're moving in for good," Joshua said, revving his dad's pickup truck.

"Unfortunately, it appears so."

"Unfortunately? Julie, you're in the heart of Zion!"

I looked at him and laughed. "Zion is a national park in Southern Utah."

"There's more than one Zion."

"Like there's more than one Blue Springs, right?"

"Zion is different. It's a location, it's a people, and it's in here," he said, pointing to his chest.

"Come on, in *there*?" I teased, tickling him near the spot he had pointed to.

The truck swerved. "Cut it out or we'll have an accident," he chided.

Joshua pulled into the drive-through lane at Burger King. After placing the order through the microphone, he put the truck in park and pulled on the emergency brake.

"Think fast," he said, tickling me so hard I slid off the seat.

On the way home, we drove past a city park. "Do you play?" Joshua asked, nodding toward the basketball court.

"I'm too short. How about you?"

"Whenever I get the chance."

"You mean you don't get it very often?"

"Not this summer. I've got too much schoolwork."

"Why are you pushing yourself so hard?"

"I'm trying to finish a full year of college by Christmas."

"Are you that anxious to become a doctor?"

A tiny smile flickered at the corner of his mouth. "No, I'm pushing myself so I can be a missionary when I turn nineteen in January."

"You're going to be one of *those*?" I thought of the starched shirts I'd seen pouring out of the MTC. For some reason, Joshua didn't seem to fit the mold. A missionary was an abstract figure. It was someone you didn't know.

"How long is a mission?" I asked.

"Two years."

"What about becoming a doctor?"

"It can wait."

"It takes eight years to become a doctor, and that doesn't include internship. If you add two more years for a mission, that makes you almost thirty before you even start your career. Are you sure you want to wait that long?"

"Positive."

Joshua was definitely among the brainwashed. I sat depressed and silent the rest of the way home.

CHAPTER THIRTEEN

The Pianist

"See you at choir practice," Joshua said, brushing past me after Sunday School.

I frowned at his retreating back. I didn't like being pushed into anything.

"Are you singing in the choir, Julie?" Derrick Van Horn asked. "I couldn't help overhearing."

"Singing? No. I'm the accompanist."

"Hey, that's great. You're a wonderful pianist."

"Thanks," I muttered.

"Why the long face?"

I looked at him. "This wasn't exactly my idea. I mean I didn't volunteer for the job. I got shoved into it."

"Oh." He looked thoughtful. "You know, Julie, teaching this class wasn't exactly the thing I wanted to do, either. But after getting into it, I wouldn't trade it for the world."

"You're a good teacher," I said.

"I'm getting better." We turned the corner and he went through a doorway into priesthood meeting.

During Relief Society, I thought about what he had said. I could use the practice accompanying others. Maybe someday I'd be the pianist for an orchestra: "Julie Edwards with the Philharmonic Orchestra." I could use the experience for the future. And the sentimentality of the music was alluring. It plucked softly at the strings of my heart. One more time wouldn't hurt, and Shirley Reynolds would probably be back on her feet in a week or two.

After choir practice Joshua walked me home.

"Congratulations," he said, opening the front door of the chapel.

"Very funny."

"Brother Roberts thinks you're great."

"Yeah, and now look what I have to do."

"Playing for stake conference is a real honor."

"For who?"

"For you!"

"I'm not a Mormon."

"So?"

"So people that aren't Mormons aren't supposed to play the piano for stake conference. "

"How do you know?"

"I wasn't born yesterday."

"Then get baptized!" he challenged.

"Not on your life." I started walking faster.

"What are you trying to do—lose weight?"

I started jogging.

"I like you the way you are, Julie."

"You're infuriating," I said through clenched teeth.

"I was only kidding." He grabbed my arm, slowing me down.

"About getting baptized or liking me?" I challenged.

"Both," he teased. "Seriously though, no one gets baptized unless they have a testimony. You don't have one yet, so don't worry about it."

"What makes you think I'll get one?"

He smiled, moving his eyebrows up and down a few times.

"I read it in the stars." He leaned closer touching noses. "The ones in your eyes."

"You look like a cyclops," I said, pushing him away.

"Are you still mad?"

I hesitated. "No."

"Will you say that a little louder, please?"

"No!" I yelled.

The lady watering her lawn across the street looked up. We both waved.

"Good." His grip on my arm dropped to my hand and he squeezed my fingers. "I have something to tell you."

"What?"

"This is pretty serious. Are you sure you're ready for it?"

"If I'm ready to play in stake conference, I'm ready for anything. Except baptism," I corrected.

"I want you to know why I'm going on a mission."

I looked at his fly-away hair and freckles. How could he be serious about anything?

"I'm going because it's true. The whole thing is true. I know God and Jesus Christ appeared to Joseph Smith. I know there is a true prophet of God on the earth today. And I know the Book of Mormon is a second witness for Jesus Christ just as I know that grass is green."

"In winter it turns brown," I said.

"Ok, that was a bad analogy."

"How about as you know the sun will set in the west."

"How about I forget the analogies. You're not making this easy for me." We walked a ways in silence then Joshua said: "The gospel has been restored and the message is going to all the world. I believe that, and I want to be a part of it."

"And I don't."

"Not yet."

"Why do you keep saying that? Why do I have to believe what you do?"

"Your grandparents do; your mother and father do."

"My mother maybe, but not my dad and not Theodore."

Just then we heard a honk and a car pulled over to the curb.

"Want a ride?" Dad asked.

"What are you doing here?" I said, opening the door.

"I had an interview with the bishop."

"What about?"

"Lots of different things."

Joshua climbed in the back next to me.

"What are you kids up to?" Dad asked.

"Choir practice," I said dryly.

"Julie's playing in stake conference next week."

"That's great," Dad said.

I glanced at Joshua. He was trying unsuccessfully to keep a smile off his face.

That night I lay in bed, but I couldn't sleep. I rationalized it was because for the first time in weeks I had a room to myself. I couldn't hear Theodore's teeth grinding.

Rolling toward the window, I stared at the movement of the curtains on the sill. Suddenly, I was back in choir practice playing the piano, watching Brother Roberts, and listening to the choir sing.

"O my Father, thou that dwellest in the high and glorious place . . ." They were singing about God. Was he *my* father too? I had a peaceful feeling inside. ". . . when shall I regain thy presence and again behold thy face?" What would it be like to see God? What did he look like? "Father, Mother, may I meet you in your royal courts on high?" If I had a father in heaven then it would make sense to have a mother too. Wouldn't it?

I folded my arms and stared at the light fixture. "Dear God," I prayed. "Wherever you are. Please help me to find the truth."

CHAPTER FOURTEEN

An Unexpected Change

At first glance, I thought the airmail envelope and foreign stamp meant a letter from Darwin. Curiosity replaced disappointment and I opened the envelope. Three pages. Not bad from a perfect stranger. It was then I noticed the pages were photocopied. Benjamin's first letter was a duplicate. The only thing handwritten was my name, the signature at the end, and a scribbled P.S. I read the P.S. first.

> I hope you enjoyed reading a copy of the experiences I've had over the past month. Cindy tells me you play the piano. We could sure use a piano player in the branch I'm in now. Singing a cappella is hard for the members. They don't have much experience.
> Elder Benjamin Patience

Experience at what? I thought, being members or singing?

That question became the P.S. to the letter I sent back to Benjamin. The rest of the letter was a photocopied story from *Seventeen* magazine. I chose one that would make his eyeballs sizzle.

"Did you get a letter from Benjamin?" Cindy asked when she saw me at stake conference.

"Yes, and I've answered it."

"Thanks a lot. I'm sure Ben will appreciate it."

"He just might at that," I said.

I took my place on the stand with the other choir members. They were singing at the beginning and end of the conference. I hoped the wait in between wouldn't be too boring. I was playing the choir songs on the piano. Another woman would play the congregational hymns on the organ.

When the choir finished their first number, I moved to an empty padded chair nearby. Unbuckling my shoes, I wiggled my toes in the plush carpet and settled down in the softness of the upholstery. There was no comparison between the comfort of these chairs and the hard benches the congregation sat on. No wonder the bishop had dozed off during sacrament meeting once or twice.

The man conducting began reading a long list of names. After each one, someone stood up. I stifled a yawn and stared at the clock on the back wall. One hour and forty-eight minutes to go.

"Dean Edwards," the man read.

I looked around. Who had the same name as my father? No one did. Dad was standing up along with several other men. In slow motion, the congregation raised their hands.

"Anyone opposed?" the man conducting asked.

Opposed to what? "What was that for?" I elbowed the lady next to me.

"Those men were ordained elders," she whispered. "Congratulations, for your father."

Congratulations? He was a TRAITOR! I was positive he had been tolerating all this church business for mom's sake, but this was going too far.

We drove home in the Toyota van Dad had bought a week after our arrival. Grandma and Grandpa were riding with us. They were both as pleased about Dad being ordained an elder as I would have been had I just received a Grammy for best song of the year. Grandma invited us over to dinner to celebrate. Mom had that goofy, contented smile on her face that she always wore at church, and Theodore asked when *he* could become an elder, too. I didn't listen to the answer. I just stared out the window.

It wasn't until lunch was over and Theodore and my Grandparents were playing Kootie that Dad noticed my indifference.

"We're playing Monopoly when we finish *this* game," Grandma said. "Do you want to join us?"

"I think I'll go pick some grapes," Dad said. "Want to come along, Julie?"

"Don't forget the basket," Grandma called as the door closed behind us.

"The basket's in the kitchen, Dad," I said as we walked down the steps.

"We won't pick that many."

I followed him around the side of the house under the trellises of hanging vines.

Dad plucked a cluster of grapes and handed it to me. "I remember when your grandpa first started growing these vines. It was about the time I met your mother. There were just a few vines back then. He didn't even have trellises. It's been his nurturing over the years that has turned what he started into this tunnel of luscious fruit."

"So, Grandpa's a good gardener."

"It's more than that. He took something, nurtured it, and made it thrive."

"Did you bring me out here to talk about grapes?"

"In a way I did."

I opened a grape with my fingernails and extracted the seeds. "Theodore has spitting contests with these," I said, dropping them on the ground.

"Where did he learn that?"

"From Joshua."

"Now *there's* a nice boy."

I looked up. "Nicer than Darwin?"

"They're different. Darwin has a lot of self-confidence. He's more . . ."

"Sophisticated," I said.

"Yes. And Joshua is more levelheaded. He has goals. He's . . ."

"Country," I added, "all the way."

"Is there something wrong with that?"

"I guess not."

"You know, Julie, you should get to know a lot of boys before you decide who you want to marry."

"I don't have any plans for marriage in the near future, thank you."

"I just want you to make sure that when you make that decision it's a wise one."

"Like yours was with Mom?"

"I love her very much."

"Is that why you wanted to become an elder? To please her?"

"In a way, yes."

"Then you don't really believe all that mumbo jumbo that's taught in church, do you?"

"I did when I was first baptized, long before you were born, but then I let other things become more prominent in my life. Since your mother's illness, though, I've spent more time thinking about priorities."

I dropped another couple of seeds on the ground and ate the split grape.

"Your mother is the most important thing in my life. You and Theodore are second. I'm willing to do whatever it takes to enable us be together forever. If it were to climb the Wasatch Front, I'd start training today."

"Dad, I have a question."

"Yes."

"Where's the Wasatch Front?"

I found out that was the name of the mountains I had been staring at since our arrival. For the next couple of weeks, every time I saw them, I thought about Dad's willingness to climb. The problem was, I didn't feel the same way, and I knew it was starting to bother Mom and Dad.

To my surprise, a week later I received a second letter from Benjamin.

Dear Sister Edwards,

I appreciate your thoughtfulness in sending me what you supposed to be a good story; however, I was unable to finish reading it. The glare from the pages hurt my eyes. I did make good use of it, though. I used it to shine my shoes for church on Sunday. Could you find something a little more uplifting and less sensual the next time?

Elder Patience

The next three pages were more photocopies of his mission experiences followed by a P.S. which read: "BOTH."

After reading the letter, I went to the store and bought a shoe shine cloth and a can of Kiwi shoe polish. I put them in a padded envelope with a short note that read:

Dear Ben,

Formality stinks. It's all right if you just call me Julie; all my friends do.

I'm sorry to hear that Panama has nothing to shine your shoes with. I have enclosed something to alleviate that problem.

Julie

CHAPTER FIFTEEN

Cousin Spencer

The twenty-fourth of July comes and goes in New York like any other sweltering summer day, but out West in the state of Utah, it's a holiday. According to Grandma, Pioneer Day became a tradition in 1847 when Brigham Young said: "This is the place." Custom dictates a parade down University Avenue and a picnic at the park. We planned to do both. And we planned to do it with relatives.

Theodore's Primary class was riding on a float sponsored by the ward. He had to dress up as a cowboy, wearing a hat, chaps, and a bandanna. He couldn't have been more excited if it had been Halloween. His teacher told him he didn't need a gun, but he took one, anyway. His rifle was more modern than the era called for, boasting a night scope and shoulder sling. His pockets bulged with caps. The Primary president was in for a surprise.

Mom arranged for her treatment early so she wouldn't miss the festivities. Dad drove her to the hospital in our Toyota van which I seldom drove since Dad took it to work every day. Grandma and I took turns driving Mom in Grandpa's car.

When it was nearing time for the parade to start, Theodore and I walked to Grandma's house. Theodore shot several imaginary Indians and Mr. Peterson on the way. Although Theodore claimed he got the Indians, Joshua's father was a clean miss. He waved to us as we started up the walk.

There was a strange station wagon parked in the driveway. I assumed it belonged to relatives.

Theodore ran up the front steps and banged open the front door, shooting everyone in sight. Two of the boys inside shrieked and plunged to the floor clutching their stomachs.

"This is Julie and Theodore," Grandma said, taking Theodore's gun away. "You remember your Aunt Jean and Uncle Bill don't you?"

I vaguely remembered them. The thing I didn't recall was the size of their family.

"We got up at four to get here on time," Aunt Jean said. "We made it from Beaver in just a little over three hours."

"It would have been under three if we wouldn't have stopped for Bobby to go to the bathroom," a boy about Theodore's age said. I found out later his name was Calvin.

Grandma introduced the rest of the family. I wondered if they were Mormons. I finally concluded that since they lived in Utah, they must be. Ten minutes later we headed for University Avenue to watch the parade.

Grandma and Grandpa took Theodore with them to drop him off at the float he was going to ride on. I rode with Aunt Jean and Uncle Bill. They let their oldest son, Spencer, drive. He was tall like his father, with light brown hair and green eyes. He even had his father's rather large nose. I sat in the back crammed between Bobby and Calvin. Their only daughter sat in the infant seat by the window.

A foul smell slowly permeated the air as we drove. Bobby leaned closer to the infant seat. "P-U, it's Melissa!"

"We'll change her diaper as soon as we get there. Sorry about this," Aunt Jean apologized.

"That's okay," I lied. I was breathing through my mouth as inconspicuously as possible. I looked at Spencer. The back of his ears were beet red. I was glad I only had Theodore to embarrass me. He had three times as many possibilities for embarrassment.

To my surprise, it was Spencer who actually changed Melissa's diaper.

"You're pretty good at that," I commented.

"What?"

"Changing a diaper."

"Nothing to it. Want to try?"

"No thanks. I'll just watch."

He deftly folded the dirty diaper and shoved a new one under the baby's tiny bottom. "Will you throw this in that garbage can over there?"

I looked with distaste at the object in his hand.

"It won't bite," he said.

"Hey, Calvin," he called, giving up. "Throw this in the trash." He threw the diaper in Calvin's direction. It landed with a splat. Retrieving it, Calvin lobbed it in.

"So you're the cousin who lives in New York," Spencer said, picking up Melissa and closing the door. We walked toward University, where a large crowd was gathering.

"I *used to* live in New York," I corrected.

"What's it like back there? I've never been east of Colorado."

"It's different. There are lots of tall buildings and the traffic is so bad people usually take taxis."

"The Statue of Liberty is in New York, isn't it? What's it like?"

"Well, I've only been there once on a field trip in grade school. It's a tourist trap."

"How about the Empire State Building? Have you been inside that?"

"Just on the ground floor. It was snowing and I wanted to warm up while I waited for a bus."

Spencer frowned. "You mean you were that close and you didn't even go to the top?"

"There are a lot of buildings in New York taller than the Empire State Building," I said, defending myself. "I've been to the top of those."

"Over here," Aunt Jean called. "The parade's almost to the corner."

I don't know what kind of parade I was expecting, but what I saw wasn't it. There were the usual high school bands with flag girls and baton twirlers, but there were no camera crews or sound systems blasting out the participants' names. There were floats with people walking alongside, but everything was on a much smaller scale than I was used to. Not even the best float was good enough to enter the Thanksgiving Day parade in New York. This rustic display would never compare to a ticker-tape parade down Broadway with confetti falling like snowflakes. At the thought of New York, a wave of nostalgia swept over me, leaving me weak in the knees.

"There's your brother," Spencer said, pointing to a tractor pulling a large flatbed trailer piled high with hay and children.

Theodore waved and threw some candy at us. Calvin and Bobby made a dash for it, knocking me backwards into Spencer. Fortunately, he had given Melissa to Aunt Jean and managed to catch me before I hit the ground.

The parade entry after Theodore's was five riders on horseback. The first one was a young man with a sign pinned on his back that read, "The husband." The next four were girls dressed in long dresses and sunbonnets. They wore signs that said Wife # 1, Wife # 2, and so on.

Darwin was right! They did have plural marriage.

"What does that mean?" I nudged Spencer.

"That guy's supposed to be a polygamist," he said.

"Are all Mormon's polygamists?"

"No, Mormon's aren't polygamists," he insisted.

"Then why are they wearing those signs?"

"Because Mormons used to be polygamists."

"Oh."

"Did Brigham Young have twenty-seven wives?" I challenged.

"About that many."

Curiosity got the best of me. "Where did he put them all?"

"You're pulling my leg, right?"

"No, I really want to know."

"Ask my dad. He's an expert."

On what? I wondered.

We didn't see Mom and Dad until the parade was over. By then it was time for the picnic. We loaded the Jell-o salad and brownies Theodore had helped me make into the back of the van with the cold cuts and chips.

At the last minute, Grandpa decided Provo Canyon would be cooler, so we caravaned out of the city and headed up into the mountains. It was amazing to see so many trees and grassy slopes with only a smattering of houses on them. If this canyon were near New York City, it would be a gold mine for developers.

As we climbed upward, the river ran along the road and then disappeared, only to reappear again in a narrower stream than before. When the road paralleled the river again, I rolled down my window and listened to the sound of the rolling water.

"Look at that waterfall," I blurted out.

"That's Bridal Veil Falls," Grandpa said.

The water fell in a narrow stream from the mountain crest, spreading wider into a light spray as it cascaded downward. By the time it reached the bottom, it had widened into a gentle mist.

Melissa was still asleep when Aunt Jean put her in a stroller. Spencer pushed her toward a shaded picnic table and I carried the Jell-o salad that was already starting to melt around the edges. We spread everything out on a tablecloth and Grandpa said the blessing—a long one in which he mentioned the pioneers and the beauties of Utah. I opened one eye and watched a chattering squirrel run up a nearby tree. Tiny yellow cowslips grew at the tree's base. The sunlight filtered through the leaves and branches, dancing across the spray of flowers in constantly changing patterns. The canyon was pretty if you fancied natural things. I worried a little that my fancies were changing.

"Pass the forks," Dad said, dumping pork and beans on his plate. After a five-minute search, which included the back of both vehicles, it was obvious the forks were still at home in a drawer.

Spencer tried a potato chip spoon and left half of it buried in his coleslaw. I used a cracker with better results. My idea caught on. Crackers started dipping into everything from potato salad to Jell-o.

When we were almost through eating, Calvin challenged Theodore to a Jell-o snarfing contest. It was too awful to watch. I sat with my back to them and threw soggy crackers to the squirrel.

Calvin finally won the contest. His whoop turned heads in the next campsite. I sympathized with Spencer; having a brother worse than Theodore had to be hard. I took a handful of chips and passed Spencer the bag.

"Are you going to BYU in the fall?" Spencer asked.

"I guess so," I said, stuffing my mouth full.

"That's great! I'm going there next year. I want to get at least one year of college in before I leave on my mission."

I choked on my chips.

"Heimlich maneuver!" Uncle Bill yelled. He jumped up and grabbed me around the waist. I thought my stomach was going to come out my mouth.

"Water," I finally gasped.

Everyone congratulated him for saving my life. I would have preferred the water without Uncle Bill.

CHAPTER SIXTEEN

Shooting the Rapids

Chiffon brushed my ankles as I glided across the ballroom in Darwin's arms. Glimpses of envious female faces blurred past. Content and confident I looked upward. His smile engulfed me.

Gradually the tempo of the music increased. I couldn't keep up. Darwin stepped on my toes. Surprised, I looked up again. His compelling blue eyes were hidden behind horn-rimmed glasses and his sleek blond hair was fly-away red. I stiffened in Joshua's arms.

"What are you doing here?" I demanded.

"Dancing."

"Where's Darwin?"

Following his gaze through the crowd, I saw Francine. I watched with trepidation until she turned, revealing the face of her partner. It was Darwin.

"Darwin," I yelled across the floor. He didn't even glance in my direction. Turning, he twirled away with Francine in his arms. "Darwin," I yelled again. It was no use. He was gone.

Dejected, I danced limply in Joshua's arms until something cold and rubbery hit me in the face. Struggling, I brushed it off and opened my eyes. The sun was still filtering through the leaves, but it wasn't as bright as it had been when I lay down on the blanket next to Mom after lunch.

"Are you ready to go?" Spencer asked, picking up the black slippery thing. He hung the inner tube over his shoulder.

"Go where?"

"Tubing."

I sat up looking for Mom. She was sitting at the picnic table next to Grandma.

"What's tubing?" I asked.

"You don't know?" His face was a study of incredulity.

"I'm from New York, okay? We don't do the same things in New York that you do here."

"Tubing is riding on an inner tube down a stream," Spencer explained. "Do you want to try it?"

Theodore and Calvin were standing in knee-deep water at the river's edge. They pushed off as soon as they saw us coming.

"Hey, wait you guys," Spencer yelled. He splashed into the water grabbing both their tubes. "We have to go together. I promised Dad."

I stuck my toe gingerly into the water. It was cold, even for a girl from New York.

"Come on, sissy." Theodore splashed water at me.

I kicked some water back at him, but hit Calvin, instead. That was a mistake. In the next two minutes, I got so wet I abandoned any idea of chickening out.

"How do you steer?" I yelled over my shoulder to Spencer. I was going down backwards, and I had an eerie feeling I was headed straight for the bushes growing along the bank.

"Use your hands and feet."

"I am!"

"You're kicking in four directions at once."

Something hit me in the back of the head and then enveloped me. I fought my way out to the end of some spindly branches and waited impatiently for the current to slowly turn my tube around. I saw Spencer a lot farther ahead than he had been a few minutes ago.

"Wait up!" I yelled.

"Push off!" he shouted back.

Even though it scratched my arms, I pulled in close for a good send-off. It was *so* good that I was at the other side of the stream in no time. I decided to stay close to the edge, moving from one branch to another. I didn't want any more back-of-the-head surprises.

The others kept getting farther ahead and finally rounded a bend out of sight. Worried, I pushed out a little from the edge and drifted into the midstream current. This time I only used my hand and foot on the opposite side from the direction I was starting to turn. It worked. Picking up speed and confidence, I rounded the bend expecting to see Spencer and company as specks on the horizon. Instead, they were waiting about twenty feet ahead.

"Keep up!" Theodore growled, pushing off again. Calvin followed him.

Spencer waited for me to float even with him before drifting into the current. "I see you figured out how to ride facing forward."

"I think I have it mastered," I said, paddling with my left hand. The tube slowly righted itself.

Spencer floated closer and pulled a twig out of my hair. "You have a few more leaves on the other side."

"Thanks." I shook my head and a bug fell on my arm. I almost tipped over getting it off.

"I see you find the wildlife quite threatening in Utah," he teased.

"Only when it surprises me."

Spencer let me get ahead of him. "Stay in the middle," he advised, "and face forward."

From time to time he called out advice to Theodore and Calvin. They were ahead of us, but we managed to keep up by staying with the current.

Shadows from trees growing along the bank rippled over the water. Our tubes bobbed from areas of bright sunlight to concealing shades of green-gray. Low-hanging bushes dipped their leaves into the stream, making miniature ripples that lengthened and spread only to lose themselves in larger ones as they headed downstream. This was the first time I had ever experienced the banks of a creek from this angle. I liked the midstream perspective.

"So tell me," Spencer said, "who is Darren? Your math teacher or something?"

"I have a boyfriend in New York named Darwin."

"That's the one."

"How do you know about him?"

Spencer laughed. "You were moaning his name when I woke you up."

75

"Come on, I was not." My cheeks burned. I didn't look back at him.

"You were probably having a nightmare or something."

Yes, I thought, a nightmare that Darwin was gone. Not only was it embarrassing that Spencer had found out about it, but it was probably true and there was nothing I could do about it.

"Rapids!" Calvin shrieked in delight.

"Where?" Spencer extended a giraffe neck trying to see around me.

"There!" I pointed, trying to get off my tube. The water was moving too fast.

"Don't fight it," Spencer yelled. "It's too late to get out. Just go with it." He crashed into me and whirled on past.

"I'm going backwards again," I screamed.

"You can make it, Julie. Just hold on."

I was half turned around when I saw Spencer hit the white water. He whooped like a cowboy. I closed my eyes and screamed as I was sucked into the bumpy current. When I opened them, a huge bolder loomed in front of Spencer. I thought he was going to become a sardine sandwich with me and the rock as bread. When he was within inches of it, he pushed off with his feet and floated on past.

How did he do that? I slammed into the rock. Water was spilling off both sides, but I didn't budge. The force of water behind me kept me plastered to the rock. Slowly I maneuvered the tube to the right. It was like trying to drag myself through quicksand. After what seemed like forever, the current picked me up and I followed Spencer downstream.

They were all waiting for me at the next shallow spot.

"We're going back," Calvin said, climbing up the bank. Theodore followed like a well-trained puppy.

"Do you want to come?" Spencer asked.

"I'll wait right here for you, thanks."

"Will you be all right?"

"I survived the rapids, didn't I?"

Pulling my tube over to the side, I climbed out and sat on the bank in a sunny spot. I was so cold from the icy water that my teeth were chattering. I rubbed my frozen arms and legs, trying to get some feeling back into them. After battling the big boulder, I was glad to be alive with no broken bones. Watching the three boys disappear among the trees along the bank, I thought about Darwin. What was he was doing on the Riviera? Even windsurfing couldn't be as exciting as my last ten minutes.

CHAPTER SEVENTEEN

Little Benny

In New York, Ruwanda had fit perfectly in the corner of our L-shaped living room. However, in Provo, with Ruwanda positioned in a room half the size, visitors usually exclaimed, "Oh, what a big piano!" Even with Ruwanda's length crowded into the corner, the conversation area was cramped.

I liked the reverberating sound in the small room. Whenever I played "The Thunderer" by John Philip Sousa, Theodore complained of an earthquake.

Riffling through my collection of music, I stopped when I saw the "Music Box." I hadn't played it in months. Simple, yet beautiful. That's what Darwin said about the song. My fingers glided across the keys. Where was he, anyway? It had been almost a month since I'd heard from him. My fingers struck more intensely, ending the song in a furious pounding.

"That's a different approach to the 'Music Box'," Mom said. Since we had moved into our new house, she had become accustomed to lying on the couch and listening to me play. "It's better than getting hooked on soaps," Mom would say. Music went hand in hand with meditation, and Mom did a lot of that.

"I haven't heard from Darwin in almost a month. Do you think he's back from France yet?" I asked. The truth was that I had gotten two postcards I wasn't counting.

"Why don't you call and find out?"

That's what I liked about my mother; she had a way of putting things in perspective. Picking up the receiver, I dialed the area code. "What if he's out with someone?" I was thinking of Francine.

"Then leave a message."

I finished dialing quickly before I chickened out. After three rings, the answering machine kicked in. I just listened to the silence after the beep. The last thing I wanted was for Darwin to come home and find a thousand messages from me on the tape. My mood changed from blue to black. I sat down again on the piano bench and stared at the keyboard.

"People change," Mom said.

"What?"

"With time, people change. Your outlook on life is based on your experiences. You may be very close to someone who is involved in the same things you are. But when you move away from each other your experiences begin to differ. Either you or Darwin may make so many changes that you will not be able to relate to each other any more."

"Utah has certainly been a change," I said with sarcasm. I didn't want to think about a change in Darwin.

"You're different since you've been here."

"I am?"

"You're more thoughtful, nicer to Theodore, and you enjoy talking to older people."

"They're my grandparents. Come on."

"It's not just Grandpa and Grandma. I've seen you talking to that old lady in a wheelchair that lives next door."

"Mrs. Simmonds? She looked lonely sitting on her front porch. Just because I said 'Hi' once she talks to me whenever she sees me. I can hardly get away from her. Did you know she has a son living in Alaska?"

"No, I didn't. How long has he been there?"

"Two years. He's working for an oil company. She's counting the days until he comes back to visit her."

Mom laughed. "You see? You're more sensitive to people now than you ever were in New York."

"There aren't any people like Mrs. Simmonds in New York, Mom."

"There are hundreds. You just didn't see them."

"So that's one person, big deal."

"Julie, you talk to older people at church."

"If you tell me that church is making me change, I'll quit going," I threatened.

"No, it's just you. You're changing and maturing on your own."

Thanks," I muttered.

"Julie."

"Yeah."

"I like what you're becoming."

The rest of the morning I spent practicing the piano until it was time to take Mom to her appointment. I avoided any piece that reminded me too much of Darwin.

In the afternoon, Grandma dropped by.

"Can the mailman come in?" she asked when I answered the door.

"That depends on whether you're bringing good news or bad."

She handed me a thick envelope. "I hope it's good."

Even upside down, I recognized Elder Patience's handwriting. He had a peculiar slant to his 't's and 'l's. I frowned, but Grandma didn't notice; she had already walked past me into the living room.

"Isn't that the Patience boy who's on a mission?" she asked, sitting down in her favorite chair next to the piano.

"What's his name again, Julie?" Mom asked.

"Elder Patience."

"No, I mean his first name."

"His family calls him Benjamin."

"That's right, little Benny," Grandma said, propping her feet on the coffee table. "I used to be his Primary teacher."

"You did!" I exclaimed.

"Oh, he was quite a rascal," she chuckled. "I remember when he used to plug the hole in the drinking fountain with chewing gum. The kids would push the button for a drink and get a wad of gum in their face instead. When it happened to the bishop, he put an end to it once and for all."

"What happened to Benjamin?" I asked.

"He just thought of some other prank to pull. He was a great practical joker. He dumped salt into the punch at ward parties and sprinkled plastic bugs on the salads. Later he was blamed for disconnecting battery cables on the members' cars during sacrament meeting. To stop that, the bishop made sure he had an assignment Sunday morning to keep him inside."

Grandma leaned back and sighed. "The last thing I remember, he was involved in raiding a Young Women's slumber party. That was just a few years ago when Clara Smith and I were working with the girls. They were sleeping out in the backyard and he and a couple of his friends snuck in and stole their clothes. The next morning socks and bras were dangling from the apricot tree. That boy always kept me in stitches."

"And he still went on a mission?" Mom asked.

"Oh, he calmed down a lot before he left," Grandma said, wiping her eyes. She looked expectantly at me.

I tore open the envelope and found what I had anticipated, three photocopied pages of mission experiences. I glanced at the P.S. on the last page. It was even shorter than the one from his previous letter. "Thanks for the shoe polish," was all it said. I handed the pages to Grandma.

"Don't you want to read it first, Julie?"

"No, go ahead. It's a general interest letter."

She took her glasses out of her pocket before she started. "Dear Julie. This past week has been the best one so far. We baptized the Meneses family, the one I mentioned in my letter of June 15th."

I chuckled. He didn't start to write to me until July. I didn't even have a copy of the June 15th letter.

"My, has that boy changed," Grandma said when she finished.

"Changed by his experiences," Mom echoed.

"You're lucky to get such an uplifting letter, Julie," Grandma said handing it back to me. "But why did you send him shoe polish?"

At church on Sunday, I stayed after class to talk to Derrick Van Horn.

"How's it coming with the Book of Mormon?" he asked. "Are you able to keep up with the class?"

"So-so," I said, not wanting to commit myself.

"You don't have to start at the beginning. Just start with next week's assignment."

"I'll try," I said, staring at the table top. "I really wanted to talk to you about a different matter."

"I'm all ears," he said, closing the door. "Now what's on your mind?"

"I need to find an article on humility."

"Is this for church next week? Are you giving a talk?"

"Me? Not on your life. I need to send it to someone, a friend."

"And it has to be on humility?"

"The most humbling one you can find."

"I see," he said. "Let me check through some old copies of the *Ensign* and see what I can find. I'll bring it by your house this afternoon."

"Thanks, Brother Van Horn. I really appreciate it."

I left class with a smile the size of a watermelon slice.

"You radiate when you smile like that," Joshua said. He walked beside me down the hall. "What's up?"

"Nothing," I said, grinning.

"Come on. No lying in church."

I stopped and looked around before whispering, "Can you keep a secret?"

"Of course."

"I'm sending an article on humility to Cindy's brother Benjamin."

"He could use it." Joshua's smile matched mine when he ducked into priesthood meeting.

After choir practice, Joshua stuck to my side like a magnet. "You're doing a great job as pianist," he said, pushing open the outer chapel door for me.

"Thanks. I just wish Shirley Reynolds' baby would hurry up and get bigger."

"Don't worry about it. You've got her beat. You play a lot better than she ever did."

"That's not the kind of loyalty I need. I'm trying to get out of doing it, not take over for her permanently."

"You could always join the sopranos. They need help."

"Not as much as the tenors."

"Hey, now you're hitting where it hurts."

"You deserve it."

Joshua took my hand and sighed. "So tell me, why are you sending a letter to good old Benjamin?"

"Because he has been writing to me."

"Why would he do that if he doesn't even know you?"

"Cindy talked him into it."

"Ah, good old Cindy."

"You should see his letters, Joshua. They're all photocopies."

"Mission experiences?"

"Exactly."

"Boring?"

"Right!"

"Lacking in humility?"

"That's why I'm looking for an article I can photocopy. I need a good long one."

"Or maybe more than one."

"That would be even better."

Joshua stopped suddenly. "Can I ask you something?"

"Sure." I was expecting an idea for the article. Instead, he stood there suddenly looking like a goldfish out of water. His mouth was moving, but the only sound he made was, "Ahhhhhh."

"Is something wrong?" I shook his shoulder trying to get his mouth to work. Beads of sweat broke out on his forehead.

"It's a . . . it's a just that a . . . do you promise to say yes?"

"Before I know what the question is?"

"Something like that."

"Just spit it out, okay. I promise to give it a fair hearing."

"Julie."

"Yes?"

"Julie, will you go out with me? I just thought that since the summer semester is over, and now I have time, that maybe we could do something together. I mean, I know you probably have lots of boyfriends back in New York, but we wouldn't have to call it a date or anything like that."

"What exactly did you have in mind?"

"Maybe we could go to a movie and out to dinner. That's all."

"We wouldn't go to any church activities?"

"Well, if you wanted to, we could."

"No, that's all right. But I think we would have to call it a date."

"We would?" he sounded disappointed.

"I'll go."

"You will?" He grabbed my hand again and we practically skipped home.

"I only have one question," I said, when we got to my house.

He looked worried. "What is it?"

"I thought you could only date members of your church."

"Don't worry about it. I've got that one figured out."

As I walked up the steps, I started to worry about what he was figuring.

CHAPTER EIGHTEEN

The Date

Friday night the doorbell rang promptly at 6:30.

Closing the lid on my blush, I dropped it back into my dresser drawer and picked up my lipstick. I imagined Joshua walking stiffly into the room and sitting straight-backed on the couch. I heard Dad's muffled voice as he asked him a question. Joshua cleared his throat a couple of times before he answered. Anybody who clears his throat louder than he speaks has got to be nervous. At times Joshua was the most easygoing person in the world, full of confidence and wit. I suspected, however, that this wasn't one of those times.

I slipped on a pair of jeans and a polo with an over-sized shirt on top. While brushing my hair, I stared at my reflection. I looked rustic, just like everyone else in Utah. I re-tied my tennis shoes before walking into the living room.

"Julie," Joshua said. He couldn't have been more relieved if I had just stopped the rope lowering him into a pond of piranhas. Awkwardly he stood up. His hair was moussed and he smelled faintly of Musk. He was dressed in slacks and a silk shirt. His Sunday shoes gleamed in the artificial light. "We better get going," he said. "The movie starts at 7:30."

Since it was only 6:30, I asked, "Are we walking?" (You could drive to any theater in Provo in under ten minutes and that included parking time.)

"No, we're going to Salt Lake. That is, if it's all right with you, Brother Edwards."

"If you drive carefully, I don't see any problem," Dad said. "Just have her home by midnight. You never know what she'll turn into after that."

"A pumpkin!" Theodore yelled.

I gave him a withering look.

"Or maybe a witch," he said, sticking his tongue out.

"She'll never turn into that," Joshua said. "She's too pretty." I pulled him toward the door before the three of them could embarrass me any more.

Leaving Joshua standing on the porch, I ran back inside for a necklace. I needed something to jazz up my rustic ensemble.

"Sorry about the pickup," he said, opening the door for me. "Dad needed the other car."

"Oh, this is fine," I lied. Even the cabs in New York were newer than this. "What does your dad use this truck for, anyway?"

"To haul manure. But don't worry, I washed it out real good this afternoon."

I sniffed the air. "You did a good job."

"Thanks. " He looked pleased.

"By the way, what movie are we going to see?"

"It's a Disney. You'll like it."

"Which one?"

"*Lady and the Tramp*. When you stopped to pet Sparky on the way home from church last Sunday, I knew you liked dogs."

"So you assumed I'd like to see a movie about them?"

"You haven't seen it, have you?"

"Not the new version."

"Good."

When we got to Salt Lake, Joshua parked the truck and took my hand. New York and Utah walked toward the theater, but our positions were reversed. I was uncomfortable as the yokel, especially with Joshua's suave look. On the other hand, Joshua didn't seem to notice our incongruous dress.

Straightening my collar, I adjusted my bangle necklace to a more prominent position.

"I like your beads," he said.

Maybe I should try to be more like Joshua.

He dropped my hand when we reached the ticket booth. "We're lucky. There aren't many people in line."

The fact was, there weren't many people in the theater, only kids— and they were everywhere. "Where are their parents?" I asked.

"Probably out buying popcorn. Want some?"

We laughed at the funny parts of the movie and had a popcorn fight halfway through. When the movie ended Joshua asked me where I wanted to eat.

"You haven't decided yet?"

"Well, yes, but after seeing those two dogs eat spaghetti, I thought maybe we should go Italian."

"On one condition: we use forks."

True to Lady and her love, we both ordered spaghetti.

"I'll bet you can't eat a noodle without using your fork," Joshua challenged.

"You go first," I said, looking around. Fortunately the nearest tables were empty.

Taking the napkin from his lap, Joshua tied it around his neck. With difficulty he sucked up a noodle from the side of his plate. It left a little red trail on his chin and tomato paste on his lips.

"Not bad," I said, wiping his face for him. "But I'll bet I can do it with no fork and no mess."

"You're on."

Picking up my spoon, I tugged a noodle loose from the pile.

"Cheater!" he accused.

"A spoon isn't a fork," I countered using a piece of garlic bread to slide the noodle into place.

"Okay, we'll make it the best two out of three. This time we each start with the end of a noodle in our mouths. Whoever sucks it up the fastest wins."

"Vacuum lips," I accused when he beat me.

We decided to quit playing spaghetti games when the waitress brought us more silverware.

"So, how did you decide on *Lady and the Tramp*?" I asked.

"It was the only one in the paper my parents had already seen."

"You mean you have to get your parents' approval before you can go to a movie? Joshua, you're eighteen years old!"

"It's safer that way."

"Safer? From what? Making a decision on your own?"

"No." He leaned across the table. "I'm safe from mind pollution. And besides, I didn't want you to think I was *that* kind of a guy."

"What kind?" Now he really had me confused.

"The kind who would take you to something vulgar and laugh about it afterwards."

As Joshua paid the check, I thought about Darwin. No matter how bad the movie turned out to be, he always stayed to the end. With my friends in New York, the more restrictive the audience ratings, the more mature they thought they were watching the film. Gore, blood, and sex were big attractions. No one except my parents were concerned about me polluting my mind. And even they only made suggestions.

As we left the restaurant, I slipped my hand under Joshua's arm. He made me feel like I stood on top of some kind of pedestal and I didn't want to fall off.

On the way home, the truck sputtered to a stop on Seventh East. "What's wrong?" I asked.

"I wish I knew." Joshua tried to start it over and over, but nothing happened. He turned on the inside light. "We still have gas," he said flicking the gauge. The arrow suddenly dropped to empty. "We don't anymore."

"What do we do now?" I asked.

"You stay here. I'll walk to the nearest gas station and be right back." He got out, slammed the door, and started rummaging around in the back. Finally he came around to the passenger side carrying a dented metal can with a spout on it.

"I'm going with you," I said, opening the door. I brought my handbag with me and slung it over my shoulder. Liberty Park stretched out in either direction. After walking almost five minutes I asked: "Aren't there any taxis?"

"In Salt Lake?"

"Yes."

"I don't know. I've never used one."

"You've never been in a taxi?"

"No, have you?"

"That's all we use in New York—taxis, buses, or the subway."

"Someday I'd like to go to New York."

"Why?"

"To see what it's like."

"Look out, New York! Here comes Josh!"

"You can be my tour guide," he said.

"You'd need one."

He reached for me, but I dodged ahead. "How about thumbing?" I asked turning around with my thumb up.

"That's hitchhiking." He grabbed my arm, slamming it down to my side.

"So?"

"Don't you know what happens to hitchhikers?"

"They get picked up."

"No, they get kidnapped or murdered."

"In Utah?"

"Yes, it can even happen in Utah."

"But I thought everyone out here was religious."

"Not everyone in Utah's a Mormon. We have our share of addicts and drunks." He smiled. "We even have a penitentiary."

"Joshua, where's the nearest gas station?" We were in the middle of the second loooong block, it was getting late, and I was getting tired. Suddenly I saw a red and white sign through the trees. "Isn't that one over there?" I started toward it.

"Hold it," he said grabbing my arm. "If we go that way we have to cut through Liberty Park. I've heard the place is dangerous at night."

"Is that just hearsay or do you know for sure?"

Joshua took one last look down Seventh East and sighed. "Okay. Where's your purse?"

"Here," I said.

"Do you still carry that Mace you told me about?"

I took it out.

"Better give it to me."

We started across the park at a fast pace.

"Do you know how to use it?" I asked.

"What?"

"The Mace."

"Sure."

"Then take the safety off."

"Where is it?"

I slowed down. "Give it back."

Just then something hit me from behind. I felt my purse strap being yanked from my shoulder and the Mace fell to the ground.

Joshua took off, chasing my assailant. "I ran track in high school," he yelled over his shoulder. He tackled the man carrying my purse.

I picked up the Mace and started toward them. Suddenly someone else grabbed me from behind, pinning my arms to my sides. I stamped down hard on his instep and he loosened his grip. Groping for his little finger, I bent it backwards until he screamed. Breaking loose, I pivoted, kicking him in the chest. Fumbling with the safety, I Maced him as he staggered backwards. He crumpled, covering his eyes.

Joshua was thirty feet away, getting his face punched in. With a flying kick to the side of the head, I toppled his attacker and then Maced him, too.

Joshua backed up slowly shaking his head and rubbing blood from the corner of his mouth. "Are you all right?" he asked.

"Brown belt, judo," I said.

"Let's get out of here."

We called the police from the gas station.

"You were pretty good back there," Joshua said on the way home. In fact you were terrific."

"A girl has got to be prepared for trouble."

"I suppose that's just a common occurrence in New York."

"Yes, it is."

"So how many times have you been attacked?"

"You want the truth?"

"Of course." Joshua's smile turned into a grimace from the cut near his upper lip.

"Once. This was the first and I hope the last."

I looked at his face in the light from the headlights of the passing cars. It was starting to swell. "I think I'll tell my Dad you tried to take advantage of me and I had to punch you out."

"Thanks a lot," he groaned. "Why don't you just say that I got this trying to save your life?"

"That wouldn't be as much fun."

"Julie!"

"Okay, I'm just kidding, anyway."

Joshua pulled up in front of my house. "I've got something for you." He leaned across the seat and opened the glove compartment. It's that article for Benjamin. I guess if I can eat humble pie, he can too."

The next morning the *Salt Lake Tribune* carried the headline "Whirlwind Attacks Thugs." Under the caption it read, "They never knew what hit them." Mom cut the article out and framed it. She put it on the wall next to the house we had pieced together so long ago for family night.

CHAPTER NINETEEN

The Heroine

D id you really save Joshua's life?" Cindy asked Sunday morning on the way to Relief Society.

"Where did you hear that?" I asked.

"Sam told me he heard it from Theodore."

"Cindy, do you believe everything a ten-year-old says?"

"No, of course not. That's why I'm asking you."

I looked around before whispering in her ear. "He had a taste of humble pie."

"Then you actually did it. You saved his life!"

"We both helped each other. He got my purse and I got the attackers."

"What happened to his face?" she pressed. "It looks awful."

During sacrament meeting an hour before, everyone in the congregation had watched Joshua. Some looked up discretely as if checking for the page number of the next song. Others stared openly, and a few of the little children pointed fingers and whispered. His right eye boasted a black and blue crescent with edges turning shades of green and yellow. His left eyebrow was a tan band-aid and the eye underneath a swollen slit. When his turn came, he had uttered the sacrament prayer through bruised, puffy lips.

Halfway through Relief Society Cindy whispered in my ear, "You're lucky Joshua likes you."

I nodded.

Why was I lucky? I leaned closer to ask, but she was staring straight ahead. Her bottom lip quivered slightly and I thought of the Young Adult party at the Stake Center. Cindy had seemed very happy to be on Joshua's team. "He likes you, too," I whispered instead.

"No, he doesn't."

"Cindy!"

"Shhhh." The lady in front of us held her finger to her lips.

After the meeting Cindy walked quickly out the door. Following her, I grabbed her arm, dragging her into the nearest rest room, but there was no chance of having a private conversation there—too many mothers and little girls. Pulling her back out, I pushed open the door to the cultural hall. "We need to talk," I insisted, hauling her up on stage behind the curtains.

"I just want you to know I'm happy for both of you," Cindy said in the semidarkness. Her eyes glistened.

"Cindy, it was only a date."

"It was his first date."

"You're kidding. Joshua's never been on a date before?"

"NOW he has."

"But what about Young Adult parties?"

"Those are group activities. That's all he's ever done, until now." Doomsday resounded in her voice. Her bottom lip started to quiver again.

"Look, if I'd known that you cared so much, I would have told him no."

"You shouldn't have told him no. He's a free agent. He can ask out whoever he wants."

"Well, maybe he'll ask you out next weekend," I said.

"I've been waiting for two years. Ever since I turned sixteen, I've been secretly hoping, but he just thinks of me as a sister."

Awkwardly I put my arms around her, letting her cry on my shoulder. Joshua with the fly-away hair, I thought, now look what you've gotten me into. I was glad nobody was around to see us.

After a few minutes Cindy whimpered, "I thought he was going to wait until after his mission to get serious."

"Serious! Cindy, we're NOT serious." I pushed her away from me in frustration.

"Did he kiss you?" she asked.

"NO."

She brightened a little and wiped her eyes.

"Besides," I said, "I've already got a boyfriend."

"You do?"

She was so elated that I continued. "He lives in New York and his name is Darwin. He's been my boyfriend for the past year."

"And you really like him?"

"Of course."

"More than Joshua?"

I knew our friendship hung on the answer to that question. I looked her squarely in the eyes. "They're as different as night and day."

Joshua walked me home after choir practice. "Brother Roberts thinks we're the Dynamic Duo."

I groaned. "That was so embarrassing." Everyone in the choir had laughed when he said it.

"He means well," Joshua said.

"Yes, and so did Sister Johnson when she asked me to teach self-defense to her Mia Maid class."

"She actually asked you?" Joshua exclaimed. He seemed almost proud of me.

"I think this whole thing is getting out of hand, don't you?"

Joshua didn't answer.

"Are you going to do it?" he asked instead.

"What?"

"Teach the class."

"Do you think I should?"

"Of course."

I looked at him. "That's easy for you to say."

"You have a talent. Share it."

"Kicking someone in the head is a talent?"

"Self-defense is a talent." He looked at me with his one good eye. "If I had your ability, I could see you with both eyes."

My laugh was infectious.

"Don't make me laugh," he begged.

He looked so funny trying to keep his face from smiling, I couldn't quit.

"Stop laughing," Joshua pleaded, taking my hand.

I thought about Cindy and sobered up.

"How long have you known her?" I asked.

"Who?"

"Cindy."

"Let's see." He did some calculations in his head. "I could safely say ever since I was five. The Patience family moved here the summer before I started kindergarten. I remember because Benjamin said he was going into second grade. I used to think he was so smart because he could read."

"And Cindy?"

"Oh, Cindy's a tomboy."

"But she's your friend."

"We've been friends for years. She's a great second baseman. Nothing gets past her. Do you play softball?"

"I haven't played very much."

"You're into the martial arts." He tried to wink at me with his good eye.

"Self-defense," I said.

"Teach the class."

"I'll think about it."

"Think about HOW you're going to do it, not whether or not you want to."

Unfortunately that's exactly what I did for the rest of the afternoon. When Sister Johnson called later for a confirmation, "yes" slipped out before I could line up my excuses. I had set myself up and it was all Joshua's fault.

CHAPTER TWENTY

Faith

Monday morning heralded the first day of fall semester. Cindy honked for me at 7:35. We both had an 8:00 class.

"See you later, Mom," I said, fumbling with the lock on the front door.

"Have a good day," she called from the couch.

"Do you remember your first day at BYU, Mom?"

"It's a little fuzzy," she confessed.

Opening the door, I stepped out onto the porch. Cindy was waiting in the '65 Mustang that belonged to Benjamin. When he left on his mission he gave explicit instructions that his car was to be driven only to keep the battery alive or in times of dire emergency. Cindy assured me that her parents agreed getting her to school and back was one of those emergencies. They planned to tell Benjamin when he came home in February. They didn't want worry to interfere with his mission.

I leaned back inside the house. "Are you sure you're all right?"

"Don't worry about me. Grandma will be here at ten to take me to the hospital."

"I'm taking you on Tuesday and Thursday. Don't forget." I had arranged my classes on Monday, Wednesday, and Friday, allowing me time on the other two days to take Mom to the hospital for her treatment.

"I'll remind Grandma."

"I forgot to kiss you good-bye." I rushed back and hugged her.

"I love you, Julie."

"I love you, too, Mom."

She had become very frail the last two months and weighed ten pounds less than what she had always termed her optimum weight. It scared me, but she made jokes about it. She said that now she could eat anything she wanted and still lose weight. Unfortunately, her nausea after each treatment made eating unappetizing to her.

"I'd better go," I said when Cindy honked again.

"I wish I could go with you," Mom said as the door closed.

I ran down the steps before I could turn back again.

Joshua opened the door for me and climbed in the back. "Ladies up front," he said.

I noted the look of disappointment in Cindy's eyes, but it was too late now to change places.

"What happened to your bike?" I asked Joshua as Cindy backed out of the driveway.

"Flat tire."

"Did you let the air out yourself?"

"Very funny. Cindy, would I do something like that?"

"You might," she said.

I gave her a thumbs up out of Joshua's line of vision.

"Now I've got two of you against me," he said. "I'm outnumbered."

"And outclassed," I added.

"First she stabs you and then she twists the knife in the wound."

I looked back at him. "Speaking of wounds, yours look worse."

The color under Joshua's right eye had deepened and the yellow-green edges were wider. The color around his left eye had blossomed to match the right. A bruise near his mouth had shown up since Sunday.

"But the swelling has gone down," he insisted. "I can see you with both eyes now."

"What a treat," I laughed.

Joshua's snicker was followed by a moan. "I asked you yesterday not to make me laugh."

Cindy sat mutely behind the wheel. We parked in a student lot and walked toward campus together. Joshua walked in the middle.

"How's Benjamin doing?" I asked Cindy.

"We haven't heard from him in a while."

"Did you mail him the article?" Joshua asked.

"What article?" Cindy said.

"The one I gave Julie."

"What article?" Cindy demanded looking at me.

"The one on humility. He asked me for some uplifting articles and Joshua said he had one."

"Good old Ben," Joshua said. He put his arms around both of us reeling us in closer. "A little humility never hurt anyone, huh girls."

This time Cindy laughed.

At lunch time we all met in the cafeteria. Cindy and Joshua were already sitting at a table when I got there. If I tried, I could be late more often.

"How's it going?" I asked, banging Joshua lightly on the head with my lunch tray.

"Careful with the curls," he said.

"You sound like a girl," I accused, sitting next to Cindy.

"There are lots of girls who would like to have those curls," Cindy teased.

"Should I get my hair cut?" Joshua asked.

"Now how would a macho doctor wear his hair?" I theorized, picking up my hamburger. "Maybe a little shorter on top and around the ears, but definitely longer in the back. What do you think, Cindy?"

"Well, a missionary haircut would be shorter all over."

The mention of a missionary irked me. "Like that guy over there?" I asked, pointing to a pair of missionaries who had just walked out of the bookstore. "With a part in the middle?" The chubby one had his hair slicked down and banked to either side of his round face.

"I like the other one better," Cindy said.

I didn't blame her. The other one was a foot taller and must have been a basketball star in Greenland before coming to the MTC. His handsome nordic features and green eyes were awe-inspiring beneath his short-cropped blond hair.

"Let's give Joshua a part," I said after they walked past. I pulled a comb out of my purse and leaned across the table. He let me fuss with his hair for a minute until Cindy produced a mirror.

After studying his reflection a second, Joshua said: "All I need now is a wad of gum to stick on the bridge of my glasses." He tousled his hair back to normal before I could find an extra stick in my purse.

"Now you look like Joshua," Cindy said. She got a smile for that comment.

"I hate to eat and run, but I have another class in five minutes."

"You've sure got your Mondays loaded, Julie," Cindy said.

"I planned it that way. All I have on Tuesdays and Thursdays is a religion class at eight in the morning." I said *religion* with disgust, but I didn't get a rise out of either one of them. "I need to help take my mother to the hospital those two days," I added more seriously.

"There isn't anyone else who can do it?" Cindy asked.

"I want to do it." At their stunned expressions I added, "I want to be with her as long as I can."

"She's going to be all right," Cindy consoled. "Just you wait and see."

"Can I walk you to class?" Joshua offered.

"No, I'm fine," I said, turning away. I wanted to be alone.

He caught me at the door. "It's no trouble."

"And Cindy?"

"She's going to the library to study. She's through for the day. So where are you headed?" He pushed open the door and we walked out into the sunshine.

"Physics 101."

"The basic of basics."

"So what's wrong with the class?"

"Nothing, if you're going nowhere in physics."

"I'm not interested in physics. I'm only interested in filling a requirement."

"Then you've succeeded. But I thought you wanted to take some music classes."

"I did, but most of the ones I wanted meet on Tuesdays and Thursdays."

"You've got five days a week just like the rest of us."

"I've got three, and if it doesn't fit in those three days I'm not taking it."

"It's your mother, isn't it?"

"Yes, and don't you breathe a word of this to her. She thinks I'm taking everything I want."

"Julie." He spun me around. "Don't you remember that blessing your mother received at your grandparents' house?"

"Yes, I do. And since then she's lost almost all her hair and almost twenty pounds. She's not going to last much longer and there's nothing I can do about it. That's why I want to be with her as much as I can." I yanked my arm out of his grip and took off across the grass. He just didn't understand.

"Physics is in the other direction," he called after me.

"So you've been leading me on a wild goose chase," I spat out as I walked back toward him.

"Will you just calm down and listen?"

I stopped and looked at my watch. "You've got thirty seconds." I didn't think I could keep from crying much longer than that.

"I wrote in my journal the promise your grandpa mentioned in your mother's blessing." He took a deep breath. "She was blessed to be made whole and well according to her faithfulness and the faithfulness of those who love her."

"Are you saying it's my fault if she dies?"

"Julie, all I'm saying is you need to have a little faith."

"In what? Something I can't see?"

"If you could see God you wouldn't need faith to believe he's there."

"Your thirty seconds are up."

His smile was lopsided. "Did I convince you?"

"You convinced me I'm going to be late for class if I continue to hang out with you."

During physics I only caught bits and pieces of what the teacher was saying. When I started to listen, I realized that physics was based on natural laws—things you could see, touch, or prove. I didn't need faith to understand physics. Why couldn't everything in life be as simple?

CHAPTER TWENTY-ONE

Darwin

"Darwin called," Theodore said as I walked up the front steps. "When?" A shiver ran down my spine.

"About an hour ago."

"What did he say?" I demanded, grabbing Theodore by the shoulders.

"He's going to call back. Don't worry."

"When?"

"You're hurting me."

"Sorry." I released him and straightened his shirt.

"He didn't say when."

"Thanks a lot, Theodore. Don't you know how to take messages? All you had to do was write down one little message." I stopped ranting. "Did he want me to call him back?"

Theodore shrugged his shoulders.

"Don't you know this is important?" I stomped in the front door, making sure it slammed with a bang.

Doing homework was out of the question. I glanced sideways at the phone, willing it to ring. Where had he been all this time? Almost six weeks had passed since he left for France. Lately, when I thought of Darwin, I got angry. Since I didn't like being irate, I had tried not to think about him. I sat down on the couch and fumed.

After ten minutes, I pulled out my study sheets from the Book of

Mormon class I had on Tuesdays and Thursdays. There were over ten pages. How many hours was I supposed to spend finding the answers? I stuck the lot of them under my physics book. I'd wait for help.

The teacher, Brother Hughes, said we were also expected to read the entire Book of Mormon by the end of the year. Fat chance. I planned to read only what was required for the individual questions. Anything hard I would discuss with Joshua or Cindy. All I wanted was a passing grade. That couldn't be too hard with a subject like religion.

I chuckled. Darwin would be surprised I was actually taking a class on the Book of Mormon. I decided to tell him it was part of my plan to get close enough to taunt without getting burned.

Maybe I should take Cindy up on her offer to meet with the missionaries. I could ask them homework questions without having to look them up myself. They'd all think they were reeling me in. At the last moment I'd flip clean out of their reach. Darwin would get a kick out of that.

By 10:30 that evening, I had given up on Darwin. I went to the bathroom for a hot shower. After slipping into my pajamas I slid between the sheets. I felt the anger creeping back again, this time coming hand in hand with a sadness I had not allowed myself to feel before.

The light coming in under my door switched off sometime after eleven. Just as I was drifting toward troubled dreams, I heard the phone ringing. Throwing back the covers, I ran toward the living room. In the dark I bumped into the coffee table. Rubbing my shin, I hobbled the rest of the way to the phone.

"She's asleep," I heard Dad say when I picked up the receiver.

"Should I call back later?" Darwin asked.

"That won't be necessary," I cut in.

"Julie, how are you?" he said as Dad's connection clicked silent.

"I'm fine. How was France?"

"*Maraveller. Je ne pour pas vous dire que maraveller.*"

"What?"

"I stayed long enough to pick up some French. What do you think?"

"Would you mind translating? I took German in school, not French."

"I said I had a marvelous time."

"You stayed six weeks?"

"Almost. My mother found an apartment near the beach that the landlord wanted to lease for a month or more, so we stayed on. I must admit it got a little old watching the surf, the sun and the local a . . . girls every day. You know the U.S. dress code is a little primitive compared to that of France. The French women are really liberated."

"What do you mean by that?"

"Well, let's just say bikinis are too modest to wear on the Riviera."

"What did they wear then, Darwin?"

"Well," he cleared his throat. "They wear something that looks like the bottom half of a bikini."

"Oh." I felt my cheeks getting hotter. Why were we talking about bathing suits?

"Like I said, they were liberated women."

My curiosity got the best of me. "Did you find one you liked?"

"One what? Bathing suit?"

"No—girl."

"Not in France. They all have hairy armpits. So what have you been up to?" he asked, changing the subject.

"I've started college."

"Already? I'm not due to start at NYU for another two weeks. How does it feel to be a big college coed?"

I thought about the Juilliard School of Music where I should have been starting in September, not at BYU. "Not as wonderful as I thought it would be."

"What classes are you taking?"

"I've got physics, religion . . ."

"Religion," he hooted. "You must be falling—hook, line, and sinker. Does that mean I win the bet?"

"No, it's a required class just like English."

"There's no way out?"

"Not that I can find."

"Well, you're definitely getting indoctrinated. Maybe I'll win after all."

"Not a chance."

His groan made my day. He didn't like loosing.

"However," I said, "I've got the answer to the twenty-seven wives question."

"What's your source?"

"My source is the real McCoy. I asked my uncle."

"He's probably prejudiced."

"If you want to find out about Italy, ask an Italian. If you want to find out about something in Mormonism, ask a Mormon. My uncle says that the Mormons used to practice polygamy just as the prophets in the Old Testament did, but it was outlawed in 1890 when Utah became a state. The only polygamists left in Utah aren't Mormons, and they're a dying breed."

"You're pretty thorough for a disinterested party," he teased.

"How's Francine?" I asked and then held my breath.

Darwin hesitated. "Francine who?"

"Francine, the one who used to go out with Dave. The one you were consoling before you left for France."

"Oh, her. I don't know. But now that you mentioned it, I'll give her a call and find out for you."

"Don't you dare."

"Do I detect a hint of jealousy?"

"No," I lied. "What's happening in New York?"

"Same old stuff. Radio City has a new show."

"I wish I could see it."

"You mean you're not enjoying Hicksville?" he said with sarcasm.

That made me mad. "My grandparents have lived here all their lives and they aren't hicks. My mother grew up here. I've even met my cousins, and they aren't hicks, either." I stopped there because I thought I might be stretching the truth. "For someone who has never been west of the Mississippi, you're sure opinionated."

"So Utah has its good points," he conceded. "What are they?"

I thought for a minute. "Utah has beautiful canyons, rivers, and waterfalls. Also blue skies, mountains, very little traffic, and breathable air. You should come for a visit."

"Maybe I should. Is that an invitation?"

"Yes."

"I'll check with my parents. If they agree, you've got yourself a visitor."

After hanging up, I practically floated back to my room. Darwin was coming to visit me. Thrilled, I climbed beneath the sheets and imagined him in Utah. We'd meet him at the Salt Lake airport. He'd be dressed in the latest fashion, with a sweater tied casually about his shoulders, wearing pants that never wrinkled. Then we'd collect his expensive matching luggage and carry it out to the van. It was not the Mercedes we owned in New York, but it would do. Even though it was a few years old, the body still looked new.

Next we'd bring him home. He would see our tiny ancient house, my mother wearing a wig, and me in the same clothes I wore my last year of high school. There wasn't even a guest bedroom for him to stay in. He'd have to stay at Grandma and Grandpa's.

The next day, Dad would need the van for work and Cindy's parents wouldn't consider Darwin an emergency, so we'd have to take him sightseeing in Joshua's father's pickup. Cindy would want to come along so there would be four of us crammed into the cab. Darwin would roll down the window and ask, "Where are the taxis?"

Joshua would reply, "There aren't any," just as a strong back wind would bring the smell of manure wafting into the cab.

Joshua would then laugh and ask, "Who dunit?" And I would turn beet red and melt into the upholstery.

Rolling toward the bedroom window, I stared out into the night. Maybe he wouldn't be able to come after all.

CHAPTER TWENTY-TWO

Finding the Answers

The second week of my Book of Mormon class held its own surprise. It was not so much a surprise in religious matters as in social. My late arrival to class had become a habit. I needed to drop Dad at the office first, so I could have the car to drive Mom to the hospital later. Dad was not used to the earlier time. I suspected he never would be.

After parking the car, I ran across the lot, slowing only when I reached the sidewalk. By the time I arrived at the Joseph Smith Building, I was out of breath. Yanking the outside door open, I hurried down the hall to my class. I hated arriving late anywhere.

As I reached for the knob, someone careened around the corner, sliding into me. Dropping my books, I fell down hard on the concrete floor. I looked up in time to see the person that had just clobbered me lose his balance. Screaming, I covered my head with my arms and tried to roll out of his way. Fortunately, most of his bulk landed on the floor next to me. When I opened my eyes, I was staring into the placid face of Fats, the boy I'd met at my first Young Adult party.

"Sorry," he said, trying to get up.

"Sorry you missed me?" I quipped. He seemed to be having a hard time so I grabbed him by the arm and pulled. "Why don't you watch where you're going?"

"I'm Freddy," he said, shaking my hand. "Freddy Flinders. Don't I know you from somewhere?"

"I believe we met briefly at a church party."

"Yes, I remember. You're the reason we lost."

"I guess we're even now," I said, retrieving my books. To my dismay, he followed me into class and sat down behind me.

"Can I see you two after class?" the teacher asked. I looked around and saw Fats nodding. Did that mean he wanted to see the two of us? We had nothing in common except walking through the door at the same time.

That afternoon I was working on physics when I saw Joshua pedaling by. I waved to him from the swing on the front porch. When he turned around, I quickly pulled out my religion homework.

"How's your mom feeling?" he asked.

"She's taking a nap. I came out here so I wouldn't disturb her. Have a seat," I said, sliding my books closer and putting the Book of Mormon on top.

"How's your religion class?" he asked.

"It's not too bad, except for all these pages to fill out."

"Oh, those are easy."

"For you maybe, but you've been a Mormon all your life. I think they're confusing."

"So what do you need help on?"

"Everything." I handed him the homework.

"This is the same class I took during summer school."

"Good." This was going to be easier than I thought.

"So what's your question?" Joshua asked.

"What's the answer to number one?"

"That one's easy. All you have to do is look up the scriptural reference." He handed me the Book of Mormon, quoting chapter and verse.

By the time we got to the bottom of the page, I was getting pretty fast at finding the verses. "There's no scripture reference for this last question. Where do I get the answer?"

Joshua laughed. "From here," he said pointing to his chest. "It comes from the heart."

"What did you learn from the attitude shown by Laman and Lemuel?" I read aloud. "They were the rebellious ones right?"

"Right."

"What do you think I should write?"

"The teacher wants to know what *you* think."

I chewed on the end of my pencil. "Give me a hint."

"You said they were rebellious."

"They were a pain in the—sorry, that just slipped out."

Joshua frowned. "What was Nephi like?"

"He followed his father like a puppy dog. Yes sir, no sir. That was Nephi."

"Not quite. Turn to 1 Nephi 2:16."

And it came to pass that I, Nephi, being exceedingly young, neverthe-
less being large in stature, and also having great desires to know of the
mysteries of God, wherefore, I did cry unto the Lord; and behold he did
visit me, and did soften my heart that I did believe all the words which
had been spoken by my father; wherefore, I did not rebel against him
like unto my brothers.

"Did Laman and Lemuel pray to find out if their father was right?"

"No."

"What were their hearts like?"

I laughed. "They were red and pumped blood."

"That's the wrong kind of heart."

"Do we have two kinds?"

"Do you want help or not?"

I nodded.

"What was Nephi's heart like?" He pointed to the word *soften* in the verse I had just read.

"If he had a soft heart, how could it be any good at pumping blood?"

"The scriptures are using figurative language. *Soften* also means pliable, ready to listen and accept. Laman and Lemuel were the opposite. Their hearts were hard. They didn't want to believe. They turned away from the truth."

I bent over my paper and started to write. When I finished I put the paper on the bottom of the pile. "Next," I said, pointing to the question at the top of page two.

"Aren't you going to let me read your answer?"

"I would, but it's between me and the teacher."

When we finished the questions, I thanked Joshua. Not only had he shown me how to find the answers, he had helped explain them.

I liked Nephi and his brother Sam, but I felt I could relate better to Laman and Lemuel because I was more like them. I didn't know at the time that I was gradually going to swing in the opposite direction. If I would have analyzed my feelings carefully after finishing those pages, I would have found that I had already started that process. I just didn't want to admit it to myself.

CHAPTER TWENTY-THREE

Humble Pie

The afternoon of the first Cougar football game I received another letter from Benjamin. I was surprised by the thinness of the envelope. There couldn't have been more than a page inside. When I opened it, one sheet of paper was exactly what I found. It was written in longhand. I sat down on the porch swing to read.

Dear Julie,

Thanks for the lesson on humility. You sent it at a timely point in my mission. Everything was going great until a week before I got your letter. I think my head was getting a little too big from all the success I was having. I was slacking off in the effort I was putting out. I just expected it to happen.

Well, it stopped happening. My companion and I had started sleeping in a little late and had been skimming instead of studying the scriptures. We didn't fast and pray before giving the discussion on baptism to a family and they turned us down. They were golden, too.

Our bikes were stolen because we were lax in keeping them locked. We missed an appointment when we went to the police station to fill out the report and haven't been able to find our investigator home since.

The afternoon I got your letter on humility, I went for an interview with the mission president. He wanted me to work as his assistant the last three months of my mission. When I told him I didn't feel worthy, he said I was just the one he was looking for. He knew I was going to work hard. I had the impression that if I would have answered any other way he would have called someone else to do it. I wanted to thank you personally for your well-chosen message. When I get home in January, I'm looking forward to meeting you.

Sincerely,

Elder Ben Patience

Cindy honked just as I finished reading, so I stuffed the letter into my pocket and ran down the steps. The three of us were going to the football game together. Joshua sat in the back seat, as usual, and Cindy drove Benjamin's car.

"How did you convince your Mom and Dad that a football game was a matter of life and death?" I asked Cindy.

"My parents are BYU alumni. They know how important the first game is. Besides, Mom needed the family car to go visiting teaching. Her companion's car is still in the repair shop. If it weren't so close to the end of the month, she would have canceled her appointments and gone with us to the game."

Joshua walked between us as we headed for the stadium. Cindy and I were so used to it we automatically moved apart to make room for him. "How's your mom?" he always asked me. "How's your brother?" he always asked Cindy.

When he turned expectantly to Cindy, I blurted out, "Benjamin's been called to be an assistant to the president."

"He has?" they both exclaimed in unison. Cindy's face was brimming with excitement while Joshua's emanated amazement.

"What happened to humble pie?" Joshua finally asked.

"Apparently it was the message on humility that got him the position. What is an assistant to the president, anyway?"

"It means you're one of the best," Joshua said in dismay.

Cindy beamed with pride. "How did you find out?" she asked after we'd found a place to sit.

"From his letter," I said, patting my pocket. Suddenly both pairs of eyes were staring at the slight bulge. I decided to let them read it before they burned a hole in my jeans trying to develop X-ray vision.

At half-time Joshua went for hot dogs, and Cindy and I stood up to stretch. It was a mistake. From five rows behind me I heard my name being shouted. When I turned around, I saw Freddy Fats waving furiously. Halfheartedly, I waved back and then sat down. I pulled on Cindy's pant leg until she sat down too.

"Who's *that*?" she asked.

"His name is Freddy Flinders. I call him Fats for short."

She glanced over her shoulder. "I see what you mean."

"He's in my religion class."

"Lucky you." She elbowed me in the side.

After ten seconds of staring straight ahead, I felt breathing on the back of my neck. I was startled to discover that Freddy and the boy sitting next to him were now in the row behind us.

"This is George Gates," he said, motioning to the guy next to him.

He looked familiar, but I couldn't place him. "Meet Cindy Patience," I said.

She smiled dutifully.

"Are you girls here alone?" he asked.

"No." I could tell I burst his bubble.

"Our boyfriend is coming back," I said.

"You both have the same boyfriend?" George asked.

"No," I said and "Yes," Cindy said at the same time.

At their confused looks we reversed our positions.

"That's what I like about them," Joshua said, walking up with the hot dogs. "They keep me guessing."

At the sight of Joshua both young men were suddenly more reserved.

"I was just wondering when Julie and I could get together to do our special project for religion," Freddy explained to Joshua. "I saw her sitting here and decided to ask her about it."

Since "next year" would be too late, I just told him "later." When he pressed me, I settled on next Saturday.

As I watched them walk away, it came to me. George Gates was

"Goat." I nudged Cindy. "Do you remember George and Freddy from that Young Adult party we went to at the stake center?"

"Huh?" she asked.

I didn't repeat the question because the Cougars were kicking off. She wouldn't have heard me, anyway.

CHAPTER TWENTY-FOUR

The Diet

Saturday morning was doubly depressing. Fats was coming over to talk about our Book of Mormon project, and Darwin called saying he wouldn't be able to make it. He had too many things to do before starting at New York University.

"Thanksgiving or maybe Christmas," he said.

"If you wait until Christmas it should be a white one," I answered. Secretly I was relieved he wasn't going to see our quaint little house.

His parting words were: "Don't fall for any country bumpkins." Although I had cringed at the colloquialism of his statement, considering who was coming over this morning, Darwin was not far off the mark.

Unfortunately, when I offered to drive Mom to the hospital, Theodore reminded Dad of my Book of Mormon project. My parents insisted I stay and wait for Freddy.

As our van rolled out of the driveway, I caught sight of Ruwanda. Because of my classes and homework, I had been neglecting her lately. Maybe music would give me a lift. I started with "Sonatina" by Beethoven. Whenever I played it, I wished Ruwanda was a harpsichord. Although I had played several keyboards in the harpsichord mode, they weren't the real thing. I played the piece with more staccato than Beethoven expected. It was the closest I could come to the twangy sound of the antique instrument.

Changing the mood with "Minuet" by Bach, I imagined myself performing in the Lincoln Center with my hair piled high, wearing a black dress, delicate teardrop earrings, and leather pumps. The audience, in tuxedos and evening gowns, was applauding as I walk on stage. A curtsey, a slight bow of the head, and I assault the keys, not too fast, not too heavy. The audience waits spellbound for the final chord. As I hit those final notes . . .

"Hey, Julie," Theodore yelled. "The Pillsbury Dough Boy is coming up the walk. Is that Freddy?"

I walked to the window and sighed. Even the great composers hadn't pumped me up high enough for this visit.

"Boy, that guy is fat," Theodore said as Freddy started up the steps.

"Is that any way to treat a visitor?" I admonished.

"You said he was fat first," Theodore accused.

"Not to his face. Be polite, and DON'T say anything about his weight."

Theodore opened the door and exaggerated a bow. "Welcome to our humble house." His smile was sickly sweet.

Freddy sat on the couch. I sat in an oversized chair, keeping the coffee table between us. "What did you have in mind for this project?" I asked. If we got started immediately, we would finish sooner. I blamed Dad that Freddy was my partner. I had gotten to school so late the day partners were assigned that Freddy was the only one left.

"My favorite story is about Captain Moroni and the title of liberty," he said.

"Was he a captain of a ship?"

Freddy looked at me, a wrinkle creasing his brow and one nostril flared. "He was chief captain over the entire Nephite army."

"Weren't the Nephites around before the Statue of Liberty?"

"The TITLE OF LIBERTY. It was like a flag. Captain Moroni tore his coat in two, wrote on it, and then stuck it on a pole."

"And that's what you think our project should be on? Some guy who wears his coat on a pole?"

"Yes, unless you have a better idea."

I didn't know enough about the book to have a better idea. The assignment was to portray an important concept taught in the Book of Mormon in five minutes or less. The more creative, the better the grade. It was obvious ours would be innovative. No one else would chose someone who ripped his coat in two.

Freddy mistook my silence as a go ahead. "Moroni's coat was really more like a cloak," he explained, "the kind that Dracula wears on Halloween."

"Then it was black."

"No, it was probably an earth tone. They used earth-colored dyes back then."

"How do you know?"

"I'm guessing."

"So it could have been black, then?"

"If it was black, the people wouldn't have been able to see what he wrote on it."

"That makes sense," I nodded, "earth tones."

It was at this point that Theodore returned. "Would you like a dish of ice cream?" he asked.

"No, thanks," Freddy mumbled. "I'm on a diet."

"Are you sure? We have Rocky Road."

Freddy looked like he was weakening.

"Make that two tall glasses of ice water, Theo," I said. "Sorry about Theodore," I apologized after he'd gone. "What kind of diet are you on?"

"It's sort of strange. My mother found it in a magazine. She says I'm supposed to loose ten pounds in three days."

"Does it work?"

"I don't know. This is my first day." As he talked red splotches began to appear on his face and neck.

"So what did you have for breakfast?"

"Half a grapefruit, a hard boiled egg, and toast with two table-spoons of peanut butter."

"You're not hungry?"

"I'm starved."

"What's for lunch?"

"A cup of tuna, two stalks of celery, and all the lettuce I can eat."

"I'll bet you're looking forward to that."

"I was planning on buying two heads on the way home."

"Don't overdo it, Freddy. Too much lettuce can be deadly."

"It can?" The splotches on his face brightened.

Theodore returned with the water, setting it down on the coffee table.

"Just make sure you drink lots of water," I advised.

"Water is good?" he asked picking up his glass. He drained it in one swig.

"Get him some more, Theodore."

After three more glasses, I asked: "Isn't that filling? And there are no calories."

"No calories!" Freddy looked pleased.

Within minutes, he stood up to leave. Obviously he had drunk too much and was looking for the polite way of not letting me know about it. However, he stopped by the piano long enough to ask: "Do you play?"

When I nodded, his face lit up. "Then this is what we'll do for our project."

Since my part only involved playing his sister's portable organ, I quickly agreed.

The way he moved down the stairs after leaving the house, I figured he was planning on stopping at home before buying the lettuce.

The following Tuesday, Freddy stopped me after class.

"So how do I look?" he asked.

I noted the big smile on his face. "Happy," I said.

He bent down and whispered in my ear, "how about thinner?"

"You lost the ten pounds," I said.

"It was really only eight."

"I see."

"You CAN see it. I look thinner, don't I?"

If you considered going from 235 to 227 thinner, I guess he could qualify.

"Hey, if losing weight makes you this happy, go for it."

"You really think I should?"

"Don't settle for eight, go for eighty."

"I don't know. That's a lot of weight to take off."

"If you can lose eight pounds, eighty only takes ten times as long."

"You know," he said as we walked toward the parking lot, "I need

"You know," he said as we walked toward the parking lot, "I need to talk to someone as positive as you. Do you think I could call you sometime if I get too depressed or tempted to eat something I shouldn't?"

Caught up in his enthusiasm, I nodded.

"Oh, I almost forgot. This is for you." He handed me some sheet music.

"'We'll Bring the World His Truth,' by Janice Kapp Perry. Interesting."

"It's a great song. You'll love it."

"You've got your part ready?"

"All I need is three minutes of music." He looked at his watch. "Got to go."

"Don't forget the organ for Thursday," I called after him. I watched him lumber back toward campus. "Jog," I yelled.

He shifted gears and his middle section started bouncing out of rhythm with his feet. He had a long way to go. I wondered if I would regret the offer I had made to be a listening ear over the next few weeks.

Freddy slowed to a walk when he reached the curb. Maybe I should make that months, I thought, in dismay.

CHAPTER TWENTY-FIVE

The Title of Liberty

"Julie and Frederick," Brother Hughes announced. "No more than five minutes."

Nervous, I carried the organ to the front of the room. By the time I plugged it in and arranged my music, Freddy had finished pulling his mother's sheets out of a paper sack. He nodded and I started playing. Walking with a mop handle for a staff to the center of the room, he stood with one hand on his hip. He wore sandals and his legs were bare from his ankles to the bottom of a melon-colored sheet draped over his shoulder and around his middle. Fred Flintstone, I thought, and missed a note.

When I started on the chorus, Freddy shook his fist in the air, saying: "Amalickiah, your wickedness will be your downfall." He pulled off his cloak, an off-white sheet tied loosely around his neck, and tried to rip it in two. Finally he used his teeth to get it started. The sound of the sheet tearing was louder than the organ and several of the girls cringed with the noise. I turned the volume up, but Freddy only spoke louder. He grabbed a magic marker off the teacher's desk and yelled as he wrote, "In memory of our God, our religion, and freedom, and our peace, our wives, and our children—"

Pulling some string from his pocket, he tied the sheet with the message scribbled on it to the mop handle. Next he put a small metal mixing bowl on his head and tied it in place with yarn attached to the metal

rings on either side. Taped across the front were the words CAPTAIN
MORONI. He hung a cookie sheet around his neck as a breastplate and
picked up a round garbage can lid for a shield. Taking the mop stick in
hand, he bowed himself to the floor and cried in a loud voice, "Bless us,
oh God, with liberty as long as there should be a band of Christians to
possess the land."

When he stood up, he strode majestically to the back of the room
slowly waving the flag. I took that as a clue to end the song. Although
I hurried to my seat, Freddy went back up front for a second bow and
the class continued to applaud. My face was brighter than his melon-
colored sheet.

At lunch on Friday, Joshua plopped down on the seat next to me.
"I hear you gave a good presentation in your Book of Mormon class
yesterday."

"You did? It's one of the most embarrassing things I've ever done."

"I heard Freddy gave a great imitation of Moroni. I wish I could
have been there." He winked at Cindy sitting across from us.

"He did a good imitation of Fred Flintstone," I countered. "The
only thing missing was Yaba daba doo."

Joshua chuckled. "Now I really wish I could have been there. I
didn't know Flinders was the caveman type."

"He's losing weight," I volunteered. "He thinks I'm his mentor in
resisting temptation from pies and cookies. Chocolate is especially
hard for him."

"How did you become his mentor?" Cindy asked.

"It was a weak moment, believe me. Now I just don't have the
heart to tell him to bug off. He calls me his positive reinforcement."

We dropped Cindy at the library, and Joshua and I continued on
toward my physics class.

"So tomorrow is the big day." He grinned.

"It's the day I fall flat on my face."

"Are you going to show those girls how to do that, too?"

I punched him. "Why don't you come and I'll use you to demonstrate on?"

"You think I want to get beat up in front of all those Mia Maid
girls? My black eyes have faded and I want to keep it that way."

"You know what I like about you?" I said.

"My sense of humor?"

"Nothing." To emphasize the fact, I started jogging away from him.

"Let's do this around the track after school," he said, keeping pace. "I didn't know you were interested in running."

I stopped abruptly. "Are you going to apologize or not?"

"Okay," he handed me his books and held his hands up in surrender. "I'll do it, but only if certain conditions are met."

"Such as?"

"No gas cans, no kicks in the head, and afterwards I take you out for ice cream."

"You're tough," I said, trying to keep a straight face. "Not even one little kick to the head?"

"Nope."

"You've got a deal." I handed him back his books and mine too. "Now let's jog. I'm going to be late."

Saturday morning Joshua came by for me in his father's pickup. Since he didn't have time to clean the back out, we drove to the chapel with the windows rolled up. He parked on the far side of the lot.

"Nervous?" he asked, taking my hand.

"I wore long pants so no one could see my knees knocking."

"Would you like to have a prayer together?"

"You mean here in the truck, just you and I alone?"

"Sure."

"Do you do this often?"

"No," he smiled. "I just thought you might like some extra help."

"Frankly, I could use all the help I can get. Playing the piano in public I can handle, but I've never taught a class before."

Joshua bowed his head.

I closed my eyes and waited. "Go ahead," I finally said. "It was your idea."

After the prayer, we hurried into the building, where Sister Johnson was waiting for us in the cultural hall. "Good. The self-defense instructor is here," she said shaking my hand. Then she turned to Joshua. "And?"

"And the attacker."

Sister Johnson had come up with what looked like real judo mats for the occasion. She had her girls sit along the edge. Joshua and I sat down facing them. Then she launched into a ten-minute speech about the importance of self-defense and being prepared. She even had a story of her own similar to Joshua's and mine about her college roommate. Last of all she read the article printed in the *Tribune*.

"With Julie's help this morning, I hope we can all become whirlwinds in the face of danger."

I stood up and rubbed my hands together. The introduction didn't help calm my nerves. Pulling a small piece of paper out of my pocket, I glanced at it and quickly stuffed it back in. What was organized thought last week looked like hen scratchings today. I glanced at Joshua. He had an expectant smile pasted on his lips.

Moving to the center of the mat, I cleared my throat. My knees were stiff from sitting so long. Suddenly I had an idea. "Lets start with some stretching exercises. Everybody up."

Sister Johnson and Joshua were the first ones to stand. We did some knee bends and waist twists. While we were doing head rolls, I remembered what I'd planned to do. "Everyone sit back down."

"An attacker usually comes from behind," I said. Joshua stood up and walked behind me. "Grab me," I cued. "If he pins your arms, you want to cause just enough pain to get released. Stamp down hard on his instep. High heels are the best, but if you aren't wearing heels, you make up for it by stamping solidly, like this." Although I stopped my thrust before I actually touched him, Joshua fell down to the ground holding his foot.

"You don't have to be quite so easy," I said, giving him a hand up.

"If your attacker still doesn't let go," I said to the girls, "and he has your arms pinned," Joshua put his arms around me, locking his fingers together, "maneuver yourself until you can grab his little finger and then quickly push backwards until . . ."

"Ouch," Joshua yelled.

". . . he screams in pain," I finished. "Then turn on him and take a jab at his eyes and knee him in the groin before running away. You want to make sure you have plenty of time to make your escape. Let's demonstrate it one more time before each of you try it."

By the time Joshua had gotten the same treatment from ten other girls, he was ready to leave. I had a feeling he wouldn't forget his participation in my self-defense class for a long time. In fact, he earned his triple-decker double-fudge sundae.

"You were great," I said, as he shoved a heaping spoonful of strawberry ice cream dripping chocolate syrup into his mouth.

He nodded and kept eating.

I licked my cone.

When he had scooped up the last spoonful, he pushed his bowl away and said: "Don't you EVER, EVER ask me to do that again. I utterly refuse. I won't do it. You could drag me down University Avenue with a team of horses, and I would still refuse."

"You got a standing ovation at the end for being such a good sport."

"I was only a good sport to save face. I have never been so humiliated in my life."

"I'm very sorry." I patted his hand and tried to look sympathetic. "If I get any more offers to teach, I'll turn them down. Although I did sort of enjoy it, after all. As I watched those girls practice what I taught them, I had a good feeling inside. I thought about what you said concerning developing talents. I hate to confess this, but I enjoyed teaching the class."

Joshua's face remained unchanged.

"However, I won't do it again. Even if they drag me down University with a team of wild horses, I'll still refuse."

"Do it again," he conceded. "Just leave me out."

"You know, I think it was the prayer," I said as we drove home.

I watched the corners of his mouth turn up slightly and knew I had scored.

CHAPTER TWENTY-SIX

Joshua Knows

Thursday morning after my Book of Mormon class, Mom was still lying on the couch in her bathrobe.

"You're not dressed," I scolded. "We're going to be late."

"I don't feel like going," she mumbled.

"But Mom, if you don't hurry, we'll miss your appointment and have to wait for another opening."

Joshua was coming over in the afternoon. I wanted to be back in time. I needed help with my Book of Mormon homework.

Setting my books down, I knelt by her side and gently stroked her shoulder.

"What's the use?" she moaned. An unbidden tear rolled down her cheek. She didn't bother wiping it away. "I hate the hospital. I hate the treatments. I hate feeling nauseated all the time, and I hate being dependent on everyone. I'm just an ugly burden on my family. I wish I'd die right now and get it over with."

Hot tears welled up in my own eyes. "You're not going to die." I hugged her, silently chastising myself for putting my wants first.

"You're not going to die," I repeated, shaking her. "I won't let you."

Mom's eyelids fluttered. She looked at me with red and watery eyes. The spider lines at the corners looked like trenches.

"How do you know? What makes you so sure?"

Suddenly I thought of the blessing Joshua had written down in his journal. "Because Joshua says you won't."

"How does he know?" Her mouth curved in a frown and her bottom lip quivered. Another tear spilled over her lashes, cutting a crooked path down her cheek.

I sat back choosing my words carefully. "He says that according to the blessing you received, you'll get better."

"Do you believe that, Julie? Do you think it's true?"

"Joshua does," I repeated. "And he ought to know."

She seemed to take heart from that and wiped at her eyes. Pulling her bathrobe around her she stood up. "I guess I'd better get dressed. We don't want to be late."

"When we get back, Ruwanda and I will entertain you," I called after her.

"Play me a little something now," she said, as she walked down the hallway to her room.

I picked up the Church hymnbook and flipped through the pages. The hymns that Mom liked best had bent corners. I usually started with "Master, the Tempest Is Raging" because I liked the ebb and flow of the storm coming across the water. Today, however, the book opened to the page before and the title "Precious Savior, Dear Redeemer" caught my eye. As I played its simple melody, I felt a soothing contentment wash over me.

"Was that first song one with a bent page?" Mom asked when she finally returned to the living room.

I shook my head.

"Bend the page, dear." She looked at her watch. "We're going to have to hustle, if we want to get there on time."

I never did anything for my Book of Mormon class without Joshua's help. That way I didn't have to spend more time studying than necessary. Today, however, I didn't have any other homework, so I picked up the Book of Mormon and started reading the assignment while I waited. As I read in Mosiah chapter three, King Benjamin began talking about Jesus Christ, the things he would suffer and the miracles he would preform. This was the same person I had played the song about earlier. When I reached verse twelve, it seemed to be written in bolder type than the previous verses.

But wo, wo unto him who knoweth that he rebelleth against God! For salvation cometh to none such except it be through repentance and faith on the Lord Jesus Christ.

As I was rereading the verse, Joshua came up the steps.

"Wo, wo unto him who is late," I said, looking up.

"A little advance preparation, I see." Joshua smiled his approval.

"So tell me about King Benjamin," I said, clearing a place for him on the porch swing.

"What do you want to know?"

"The answer to number one." I handed him the worksheet.

"Somehow you seem to make me feel like a cow."

"How's that?"

"You're always milking me for answers."

"Mooo," I said.

He mooed back.

"Let's put the cows out to pasture," I laughed. "Mom's taking a nap."

When we had finished the fourth page, Joshua suddenly asked: "Have you ever been bowling?"

"Not for years."

"Then you don't know much about the game," he said with enthusiasm.

"I used to bowl on a league when I was thirteen."

"Were you very good?" he asked, suddenly serious.

"We never took first place if that's what you mean. All we ever won was second. Mom always said if there were fourteen teams in the league instead of fifteen we'd have taken first. But I can't imagine the Bolleretts dropping out, can you?"

"Why did you stop bowling?"

"I was always more interested in music. I probably couldn't score much over 150 now without practicing."

Joshua pursed his lips. "How about archery?"

"You mean like Robin Hood?"

He nodded.

I shook my head.

"Saturday morning at eight," he said. "I'm taking you shooting."

CHAPTER TWENTY-SEVEN

Archery Lessons

The early morning air was crisp and cold as I stepped out on the front porch to wait for Joshua. Shivering, I zipped up my parka and bounced down the steps. The lawn crunched cold under my feet. I felt like walking and started down the street toward his house. An icy breeze whipped a strand of hair across my face. Tucking it back in place, I shoved my hands deep into my pockets. New York was concrete everywhere. I crunched onto the cold frozen grass lining the sidewalk. My feet sank through the top layer, leaving prints as I walked. I'd never been here in wintertime. How cold would Provo get?

Joshua honked and made a U-turn.

"Did you forget we had a date?" he asked, pulling alongside me.

"I was walking over to your house," I said.

He grinned. "Let me get the door for you."

"Where are we going?" I asked, as he pulled onto a dirt road heading out across the desert.

"To my favorite hill."

"You mean there's no archery alley in Provo?"

"What's an archery alley?" he asked.

"You know, like bowling alley."

"I've never seen one."

"Then where do you shoot arrows?"

"At my favorite hill."

"And where's that?"

"Over there." He motioned vaguely with his right arm.

"Then why are we going this way?"

"We have to stay on the road, silly."

What road? I thought, as we bumped along. It was like riding a bucking horse in slow motion. I buckled my seat belt and hung onto the armrest. I stared at the sagebrush as he chattered on about bow hunting with his dad. At least the day seemed to be getting warmer as the sun rose higher.

Thirty minutes later we dipped into a gully, ran over a large rock that sounded like it ripped the bottom off the truck, and rolled to a stop.

"Where are we?" I asked.

"At the best archery sight in northern Utah."

A mound of dirt rose off the desert floor to a height of no more than twenty feet above our heads. A few sage and mesquite bushes dotted the sparsely covered surface. At least the ground between us and the hill was level.

As I stared at the knoll in dismay, Joshua was busy in the back of the truck. He handed me a large, round object and I followed him toward the mound of dirt. Intrigued, I watched as he constructed a crude target with metal legs. He hung the target I had carried on a bulky cushion of matted straw. The concentric circle nearest the center had been torn to shreds by arrow tips.

When we got back to the truck, he gave me his younger brother's bow. Robin Hood and his merry men out for a little shooting practice. I plucked the string warily.

Joshua's bow, however, didn't look like it came from Sherwood Forest. Until now, I'd thought bows were moon shaped with a simple string connecting the two ends, like the one I carried. His had the curve and the string, but it was bigger and more ornate with a balancing rod and sighting mechanism. He slung a quiver of arrows across his shoulder and handed me mine.

"If you're Robin Hood, who am I? Friar Tuck or Little John?"

"Maid Marian," he said without hesitation.

"She never shot a bow."

"He taught her how to later."

I trailed behind him toward the target. We stopped about twenty feet away.

"Shouldn't we get a little closer?" I asked.

"This *is* close. As soon as you get the hang of it, we'll back up."

He gave me his brother's bow for a reason. Even though he said it was only a twenty-pounder, I could barely pull it back. My first arrow fell off the string. The second went halfway to the target. The third zinged over the hill, but the vibration of the string struck my arm, making me drop the bow.

"Curve your arm like this and keep it tense until your arrow strikes the target." Joshua demonstrated perfect form, letting three arrows fly into the bull's-eye.

"It looks easy when *you* do it."

"You can't miss from this close. Unless," he amended, "you've never done it before."

If that was supposed to make me feel good, it didn't work. I sent three arrows into the side of the hill and one more over the top before I finally hit the target, ripping a small piece off the outside edge.

"I hit it!" I yelled, jumping up and down.

"Now do the same thing again," Joshua said. "Only hold the bow steadier and take a deep breath before you let fly."

The last two arrows from my quiver landed in the outside ring.

"Not bad, huh?" I slugged him in the arm as we walked toward the hill to collect the arrows. Mine were spread all over the hillside. It took ten minutes to find the two that had flown over the hilltop.

Joshua commented, "I think I need a taller favorite hill." I slugged him again and slung the quiver over my shoulder. If I looked more the part, I might be able to shoot better.

We backed up to thirty feet and started again. This time half my arrows hit the target, with one landing near the bull's-eye. After I shot mine, Joshua backed up to fifty feet and shot rapidly in succession at the target and then at designated bushes on the mound.

"What was that for?" I asked.

"You never know where or when you'll see a deer. I just pretend that certain bushes are game."

"Have you killed an animal with your bow?" I asked, suddenly repulsed by the thought.

"I got my first deer last year."

"How could you stand to kill a poor defenseless deer?"

"Somebody has to do it."

"Why?"

"Because there aren't any more wildcats. The deer herds would get too big without a natural enemy. They'd eat the fields and orchards. They'd become a menace to society."

"And men aren't?"

"Men are the biggest menace of all. Look what we've done to the atmosphere and the water. Look what men do to each other. That's why I'm going on a mission."

"To hunt down the bad guys?" I razzed.

"In a manner of speaking. If everyone can develop a Christlike love, we'll treat each other better and respect nature more, too."

"You honestly believe the gospel of Jesus Christ has an answer to everything, don't you?"

"Yes."

I gathered my arrows and backed up another five feet. This time the arrows landed either near or on the target. "You can be good at something and not use it to kill with," I said.

"When was the last time you ate steak or chicken? That was a poor defenseless little animal, too. Except for one thing; it was locked up in a cage before it was butchered. The deer I killed had a sporting chance."

"But you enjoyed killing it."

"It was a goal I set for myself. I wanted to get my own deer. And to be honest, the feeling I had when I actually hit it was the most exhilarating feeling I've ever felt in my life. But I didn't get a clean shot. The arrow skimmed a tree branch and veered off its mark. I stalked the deer for two hours following a trail of blood. When I finally caught it, I couldn't handle it. The deer was lying in a pool of blood staring blankly at me. My dad had to gut it for me." Joshua spun around to face me. "And the answer is no, I didn't enjoy killing the deer. It turned out to be one of the most gruesome moments in my life."

Anguish surfaced in Joshua's brown eyes and then just as suddenly disappeared. My anger melted and I squeezed his shoulder. "It could happen to anyone. We all have goals we think we want, and then when we finally achieve them, they turn sour."

On the way back to town, I thought about Juilliard and my goal of attending. Could it have ended up like Joshua's deer, if I'd have chosen Juilliard instead of Mom? I didn't think so, but then again, I wasn't sure.

CHAPTER TWENTY-EIGHT

The Track

Halloween in New York meant staying inside and locking the door. In elementary school there had been a costume parade, but by the time I hit junior high, all that kiddie stuff was behind me. That's why having to go in costume to the Young Adult Halloween party at the stake center was such a surprise.

Joshua suggested Raggedy Ann and Andy, but the thought of wearing a dyed mop on my head all night didn't hold much appeal. Mom offered to let me wear one of her wigs, but changed her mind when I talked about going as a punk rocker. She was afraid the back-combing would give her wig split ends and that the spray-on dye wouldn't come out. Since I wasn't crazy enough to do that to my own hair, I had to come up with another idea.

In the cafeteria on Friday a week before Halloween, the three of us decided to go as the three little pigs. Cindy said she could get some pig noses. Joshua had some salmon colored T-shirts his mother had bought on sale. I couldn't come up with anything better, so it was a go.

"Julie's, at six," Joshua said.

I hoped an hour would be enough time to transform us into storybook characters.

"How's it going?" Freddy asked, sitting down next to me. He had a large chef salad and a glass of water on his tray. I felt guilty eating french fries smothered in ketchup and pushed them aside.

"Are you going to eat those?" Joshua asked.

"No."

"Good."

I looked away as he crammed my cold fries into his mouth.

"Do you always eat your salad dry, Freddy?" Cindy asked.

"It's better for you," he mumbled.

"So how's the diet going, Fred my man?" Joshua asked.

Freddy shrugged and color blotches started appearing on his neck.

"What are you going to be for Halloween?" I asked Freddy, kicking Joshua under the table.

"It's a secret," he said, concentrating on his salad.

"We're going to be the three little pigs," Cindy confided.

Freddy raised his eyebrows and stared at her.

"You could always be the big bad wolf," she suggested.

"Thanks, but I've already decided what I'm going to be."

"See you later," I said, standing up. "I've got a class in five minutes."

Freddy crammed the last of his salad into his mouth and followed me. "I've started jogging," he said, pushing the door open for me.

"How do you like it?"

"I hate it while I'm doing it, but I feel great afterwards."

"Keep it up. Jogging is good for your heart and lungs."

"Would you like to jog with me sometime?"

"I'm not a jogger. Joshua, he's your man for jogging."

"He's good at it, isn't he?"

I nodded.

"Then he's the last person I want to jog with."

"I see what you mean. When do you run?"

"Every afternoon around four at the track. I'm almost up to a mile," he said with pride.

"I'll see what I can do," I promised.

He smiled. "I'm not hungry when I'm around you."

I had never had a compliment quite like that before. I watched him walk away, and somehow there didn't seem to be quite so much about him that bothered me.

The day before Halloween, I got a letter from Panama. Actually it was really just an envelope with a scrap of paper in it.

Dear Julie,
    Your letter,
    Though light as a feather,
    Would make me feel better.
    Don't keep me waiting forever!
        Benjamin

I stuck it in the edge of my mirror and looked around for some stationery. That brother of Cindy's sure had a way of making me feel guilty. I had planned to write back. I just hadn't gotten around to it.

I pulled out some scratch paper. One good poem deserved another. I sharpened my pencil and started composing.

Dear Benjamin,
    Don't write me a letter,
    As light as a feather.
    You can do better.
        Julie.

I included a second page which talked about the Cougar's football wins and losses, the self-defense class I taught, and bow shooting. I mentioned Joshua only once. The last page was a photocopy of an article in the most recent issue of the *Ensign*.

He doesn't deserve this, I thought, as I opened the mailbox. I dropped the letter in, anyway. On the way home from the post office, I stopped by the track. I was curious to see if Freddy was jogging. A solitary figure moved tortoise-like among the hares. When he got closer, I jogged onto the track.

"Road hog," I said, coming up behind him.

"Julie!" he exclaimed, sweat trickling down his face in spite of the chill in the air.

"How many times around?" I asked.

"This is my fourth and last," he panted.

"Good. I think I can make it that far if we go slow."

Freddy plodded on with determination.

After the first hundred yards or so, my legs began to ache. I felt as if I were running on wooden blocks. No wonder I never liked jogging.

I was as exhausted as Freddy looked when we reached the end.

"That was your fourth time?" I asked.

"Yeah." He leaned forward with his hands on his knees gasping for breath.

"Congratulations," I said.

He nodded. When we reached the fieldhouse he asked, "Can I buy you a drink?"

The water from the drinking fountain felt cool as it trickled down my throat. When it was his turn, Freddy dipped his whole face in the stream and then used his shirt sleeve for a towel.

"Thanks for coming," he said.

"It was a good workout."

"Do you want to do it again sometime?"

"My legs ache so badly from only one lap, I don't think I want to make a career out of it."

"It's your shoes. You're wearing loafers."

I looked down at my feet. "I was coming back from the post office when I decided to stop by."

"I'm glad you did." He moved toward me.

I looked at my watch. "I've got to be going. My dad's off work at five and I need to pick him up."

"See you tomorrow at the Halloween party," Freddy said.

As I walked to the car, I wondered whatever possessed me to stop at the track in the first place.

CHAPTER TWENTY-NINE

King Kong

When Mom learned I was going to the Halloween party as one of the three little pigs, she decided to help out. Friday after school there were three curly tails and three sets of pink pig ears sitting on the dining room table.

"I want to be a pig for Halloween, too," Theodore said. He slipped on a set of ears and pinned a tail on the back of his T-shirt.

"Mom, can I be a pig for Halloween?" he asked, parading into the front room.

It was worth watching Mom's eyes light up while Theodore made a fool of himself.

"I'll loan you my costume," I promised.

"How come I can't get dressed up tonight, too?" he whined.

"Because tomorrow is Halloween. Tonight is just a party for the Young Adults," I explained.

"I'm going over to Sam's house right now to see if he wants to be a pig, too." He slammed out the front door and was down the steps before I could stop him.

"It looks like I've raised a couple of porkers," Mom chuckled.

I shrugged. "I'm glad my friends from New York aren't here to see me dress up like a member of the *Suidae* family."

"I thought you had forgotten about your friends."

"Sometimes I do for days at a time. Then I get involved in something really strange like this Halloween party and I think to myself, would a swine make it in New York City? Not in my old high school, it wouldn't." I sighed. "If everyone isn't dressed in costume tonight, I'm not getting out of the car."

My threat was made in vain. Most of the costumes were so creative they put ours to shame. There were even two adult chaperons dressed as Abbot and Costello.

Joshua handed me a cup of foaming witch's brew. It turned out to be punch bubbling with dry ice and plastic spiders. I dropped a sticky black widow down his back when he wasn't looking. He got me back later with a tarantula. We both put our spiders from our next cup down Cindy's back.

Joshua danced the first dance with Cindy, the next with me, then asked several other girls. I danced with a prince, Dracula, and Frankenstein. About an hour into the party, I noticed King Kong dancing with Barbie.

"Who's that?" I nudged Cindy.

"I can't tell with all that makeup on."

He was wearing a black tuxedo, white gloves and a realistic gorilla headdress that was covered with kinky black hair. His gloved fingers clutched a Barbie doll. Her eleven-inch stature gave King Kong the illusion of realism. He had a swinging gait and his muscled physique filled out his tux in all the right places. Barbie was held captive, but who was her captor? Throughout the rest of the evening, I kept glancing at him. There was something familiar I just couldn't place because everything else about him was so strange.

I was on my fourth cup of foaming bug juice when King Kong asked me to dance. Handing my cup to Cindy, I followed him out on the floor.

"I'm Julie Edwards."

"I know," he growled in a deep throaty voice.

"Who are you?"

"King Kong." His tusklike canine teeth flashed.

"No, What's your real name."

He either didn't hear or pretended not to. King Kong pointed to his ears and shook his head. Then he did a complicated dance step, threw Barbie in the air, spun around and caught her just as she was heading for disaster. I couldn't believe it. I'd never danced with King Kong before, or for that matter, Barbie either.

When the song ended, Joshua whisked me away before I had a chance to ask King Kong any more questions.

"Who is that guy?" Joshua whispered in my ear as he pulled me close for a slow dance.

"Jealous?"

"I'm not the jealous type."

Needless to say, Joshua didn't move far from my side the rest of the evening.

On the way home, Cindy asked, "Who was the mystery man?"

"You mean King Kong?" Joshua blurted out.

"*You* danced with him," I nudged Cindy. "Didn't you find out?"

"I thought *you* knew," she said.

After dropping Cindy at her house, Joshua stopped the pickup in front of mine. Instead of getting out and opening the door for me like he usually did, he turned toward me, putting his arm on the back of the seat. "I've never been this close to a pig before."

He said it so seriously, my pig snout shook with laughter. When I was under control, he leaned toward me rubbing his pig nose against mine.

"That's the way pigs do it."

"Do what?" I whispered.

"Kiss," he said.

"How do you know?"

"I learned on a farm."

I backed away. "I did an in-depth research paper on the *Suidae* family for biology my junior year, and I never found that in any reference book."

"Have you ever been to a farm and watched pigs frolic?"

"You're not serious."

"Look, Julie. Even though you're from New York, you still don't know everything. There are some things you have to learn from experience."

"Like what?" I challenged.

"Like how pigs frolic or how to shoot a bow and arrow or even whether or not the Church is true."

"I knew you'd get around to mentioning the Church. How can you be so sure it's true?"

"I feel it inside. I searched for the truth and I found it." He shook me. "Have you done your search? No!" he answered for me. "And why haven't you? Because you don't take anything seriously," he answered again. "Do you pray about it?" he asked, pointing a challenging finger at me. "Well, *do* you?"

"Do I get to answer that question myself or do you want to answer it for me?"

He opened his door and stomped around to my side.

"YOU are impossible," he said, taking my hand as we walked toward the front porch.

"Do pigs hold hands?" I asked.

"Sometimes," he glared at me.

When we reached the top of the stairs, I saw the curtains move apart in the living room window.

"Theodore," I mumbled.

Joshua turned around. With both of us staring at him, the curtain dropped quickly back into place.

"What's he doing still awake?" Joshua asked.

I shrugged. "Thanks for a good time," I said, slugging his padded stomach.

"My good-time girl." He looked at me so intensely I thought for a moment he was trying to see inside my soul. Then he gave me a half-hearted bounce with his padded middle and turned away.

That night I lay in bed staring at the darkened light fixture. Nobody had called me a "good-time girl" before. I had substance. I wasn't a flash with no depth. I folded my arms. "Dear God," I prayed, "what is truth and where can I find it? If Joshua has it, let me see it." After saying "Amen," I rolled onto my side and stared out the window. See, I thought, I do too pray about it.

On Monday, a grinning Freddy joined us for lunch. "How did you like my Halloween costume," he asked.

"Who were you?" Cindy said.

His whole face lit up. "Don't you know?"

"You were the grizzly bear, right?" Joshua guessed.

Freddy laughed so hard his belly shook. "I'll give you a hint. I was dancing with the shortest blond in the Stake Center."

"Was that Lisa Huntington?" Cindy asked.

Suddenly I slapped the table. "No, the shortest blond was Barbie."

"Barbie who?" Cindy said.

Freddy and I both laughed so hard tears rolled down our cheeks. When Joshua joined in, Cindy stared at us in frustration.

"This is the mystery man, King Kong," I said, patting Freddy on the back.

"King Kong? But how did you get so . . . so thin and so muscular?" Cindy blurted out.

Freddy leaned back, putting his hands behind his head. He grinned as if he were about to reveal the secret of the *Planet of the Apes*. "I used Inst-a-muscles and a corset."

Freddy and Joshua left the cafeteria talking about Inst-a-muscles, and Cindy walked me to physics. "You know there's a girl's choice dance coming up," she said. "I was wondering who you wanted to ask."

"Girl's choice dance? Isn't that almost a month away?"

"No, it's only three weeks and four days."

"I haven't even thought about it," I answered truthfully. But now that Cindy mentioned it, I was sure I knew who she wanted go with. She just didn't want to step on my toes.

"Who do you want to take?" I asked.

"Oh, I don't know."

I stopped walking and looked at her. "Does his name start with a 'J'?"

"Who, Joshua? He likes you."

"So what? He likes you, too."

"Are you sure? I mean, if you want to ask him, I'll back off."

"I don't know who I want to go with. Maybe I'll take King Kong."

Although we laughed at my suggestion, during physics the thought of going to a dance with Freddy Flinders kept crossing my mind. What if he wore his Inst-a-muscles and a tuxedo?

CHAPTER THIRTY

Black Ice

Friday night Darwin called. As we talked, I stared at the worn spots on the carpet—worse near the kitchen and by the front door. There had been talk of recarpeting the whole house, but with Dad's new business and hospital bills, the idea was on the back burner. I closed my eyes, imagining myself in Trump Towers, before inviting Darwin to the girl's choice dance.

"The Saturday before Thanksgiving sounds good," he said.

"Great."

"I really miss you, Julie."

"I can hardly wait to see you, Darwin."

I was still walking on clouds when Cindy came by the next morning. "Darwin's coming," I confided.

"Darwin who?"

"My boyfriend from New York. I told you about him. Wait until you meet him. Dad says I can buy a new dress, something really fancy. The only problem is that this isn't New York, and I have to find something sensational. Do you know where any really nice dress stores are?"

"Well, maybe over at the mall."

Dad and Mom dropped us off on the way to the hospital.

"If I can't find anything here, I'm looking in Salt Lake. You don't know how much this means to me."

Cindy's lips were a thin line. "I don't think I do."

I laughed and grabbed her arm. "Let's hurry. We've only got four hours."

I swirled out of the dressing room in blue chiffon and lace.

"You look like Merry Weather," Cindy said.

"Is that good or bad?"

"She was one of the good fairies in *Sleeping Beauty*."

"Then I look a little plump," I frowned.

The next dress was a cotton print of pastel roses.

"Too pale," Cindy counseled.

My reflection in the mirror confirmed her opinion.

Five stores later, I found the prefect dress. It was a stronger tone than I normally wore, but the deep plum color brought out a glow in my cheeks. The full skirt and sleeves created the illusion of an hourglass figure.

"What do you think?" I asked Cindy. She gave me a thumbs up. "So what are you going to wear to the dance?" I asked, hugging the box to me as we left the store. "And who are you going to take?"

She shrugged. "I guess I can't leave Joshua sitting home alone for an important event like this."

"You mean you haven't asked him yet?"

"I will now," Cindy said.

"Atta girl." I hugged her. For a moment I was sincerely happy for her. We ordered frozen yogurt to celebrate. However, as I sat on a bench staring at the fountain, I thought of Joshua's agony as he told me about killing his first deer, and I felt his pig nose touch mine.

"What's wrong?" Cindy asked.

"Nothing." I shook my head and a cloud of depression settled over me as thick and gloomy as smog on a windless day in New York.

Darwin's flight was scheduled to arrive at 3:00 P.M. Saturday. The dance was at 8:00.

Mom changed her appointment at the hospital to avoid two trips to Salt Lake. When she finished, we still had more than an hour to wait. As we drove past Temple Square, Theodore spotted an open parking space. Dad swerved in before I could object. *Trolley* Square was more what I had in mind for killing time.

I hated museums, but it beat sitting in the car. I lagged behind as my family walked through the gate.

"What's that big oblong building?" Theodore asked.

"That's the Tabernacle," Mom said. "It has one of the biggest pipe organs in the world."

"Would you like to see it?" Dad asked, looking at me.

"May as well," I mumbled.

Theodore ran ahead and yanked on the door. Against my better judgment, Dad had let him come with us to pick up Darwin.

As I stared at the pipes covering the entire front wall from floor to ceiling, my thoughts turned to Ruwanda. An organ that size even put *her* to shame.

When we were outside again, Theodore pointed in the direction of a large grey building. "That's the temple with the angel Moroni blowing his trumpet." A distant gold figure stood on top of the tallest spire.

"Why is a temple important?" Mom asked Theodore.

I was surprised at his thoughtful expression.

"It's important because we can become a forever family in it," he said.

I snickered, but Mom ruffled his hair and hugged him. She always was the sentimental type.

As I followed my family up the walkway leading to the second story of the Visitors' Center, I touched the wall where a star sparkled. Just paint, I thought, but from a distance it looked real.

Theodore ran over to the immense statue of Christ that stood in the center of the second-story room and touched the large marble feet. "See, this is where the nails went in." His fingers lingered over the indention. "Want to feel?" he asked me.

I shook my head. The realism of the statue gave me an eerie feeling. I turned and stared out the window at the Tabernacle. It didn't seem so large from here.

We got caught in traffic and arrived late at the airport. Quickly I brushed my hair one last time as Dad pulled up in front of the terminal.

"You go find him," Dad said. "We'll park and be right behind you."

I scanned the incoming flight board for his plane. The flight number was still blinking. By the time Mom and Dad found me, most of the passengers had disembarked.

"He still hasn't gotten off," I frowned.

When the stewardesses came out pulling their flight bags, I felt sick. Dad confirmed with them there was no one left on the plane. We spent another thirty minutes checking at various counters to see if he had even boarded. All we drew was a blank.

"Maybe he was held up in traffic," Mom consoled.

"We'd better call him," Dad said.

There was no answer. I sat silently on the way home listening to Theodore invent reasons why Darwin wasn't on the plane.

"Maybe he was carrying so many bags he couldn't see where he was going and he fell down an open sewer hole and broke his leg. Then he couldn't climb back out and nobody could hear him yelling because of the noise from the overhead traffic. So he started to drag himself through the underground tunnels until he was so lost that only the crocodiles could find him. They came snapping after him biting off his broken leg and . . ."

"Make him stop, Dad," I demanded.

"Theodore! You're not making your sister feel any better."

I checked the message unit on the phone when we got home. "I'm sorry I can't make it, Julie," Darwin said. "I slipped on some black ice this morning and sprained my ankle. It's really a bit more than sprained. It's immobilized, and I'm in the hospital until tomorrow for observation."

Escaping to my bedroom, I slammed the door behind me. Grabbing my dress, I flung it across the room. It landed on the bed and slid off on the floor. I pounded the dresser with my fists and wiped at my eyes.

Theodore knocked on my door.

"What do you want?" I bellowed.

"Well, I just thought that if you really wanted to go to the dance, maybe you could take me."

Julie and her kid brother. The top of his head only came to my shoulder. "That's a good one," I said. "Thanks for the offer, but I guess I'll just stay home."

No Darwin and no Joshua, either. For a girl who had more than her share, I was suddenly on the outer edge of nowhere. Well, at least Cindy would have a good time. And Joshua? I wondered what kind of time he would have.

CHAPTER THIRTY-ONE

Canned Chili

Cindy slid onto the bench next to me just seconds before the bishop stood up to conduct sacrament meeting. "We missed you at the dance last night. Where did you and Darwin go?"

"Nowhere."

"You mean you stayed home?"

"I stayed home. Darwin stayed in New York."

"He stood you up?"

"He's in the hospital."

"WHAT? Is he all right?"

"Shhhhh!!!" the lady behind us said.

"Sprained ankle," I whispered.

After sacrament meeting Cindy walked ahead of me for Sunday School and took the empty seat next to Joshua. I sat behind them on the back row. They really did make a cute couple, the striking blond and curly headed Robin Hood. They even shared their scriptures. When the lesson ended, I wasn't even sure what it was Brother Van Horn had been trying to teach.

After the closing prayer, I bolted for the door. Although I heard Joshua call my name, I kept going. The last thing I wanted was questions from him. I had seen enough of Cindy and Joshua together. I hurried down the hall, past the Relief Society room, and out the front door. I wanted to be alone.

The cold felt good on my cheeks, but the rest of me shivered. I buttoned my coat, stuffing my hands in my pockets. After the first block, I slowed down. Why did I keep going back to church, anyway? I didn't believe in it. They were all brainwashed.

I kicked a rock from the sidewalk into the street. I missed New York. What I wouldn't give to go back and take a taxi down Broadway. It was too bad I wasn't holding the airplane ticket instead of Darwin.

By the time I got home, my toes were numb. I stomped up the steps and looked under the mat for the spare key. When I didn't see it, I shook the mat and searched in the cracks along the edge of the porch. Sitting down on the swing, I took off my shoes and rubbed my frozen toes. Patent leather wasn't made for winter. I still had thirty minutes before church was over. I could walk back or wait outside on the swing.

By the time my family got home, my fingers were numb, too.

"Where's the spare key?" I growled.

It was sitting on the table next to the phone.

"That'll teach you to put it back under the mat," Theodore needled.

I gave him a smoldering look and escaped to my room before I exploded. When Dad finally rousted me out to make lunch, I opened a couple of cans of chili and a package of tortilla chips.

"Mexican food," Mom said, hefting a heaping spoonful to her mouth. "Thank you, Julie. I had a craving for this kind of food today."

That really made me feel guilty. The one day a week that Mom didn't feel as nauseated as usual and I fixed her a canned lunch.

"Why don't you call Darwin and find out how he is?" she suggested.

"Good idea," I said, standing up.

"After you're through eating," Dad amended.

As I dialed his number, I belched from gulping spicy food.

"How's your ankle?" I asked.

"Elevated. Sorry about the dance," Darwin apologized.

"Don't worry about it." I kept my voice light, but I was glad he couldn't see my face.

"I want to make it up to you."

Impossible, I thought.

"I talked to my mother this morning. She thinks it's a good idea."

"What is?"

"To use the plane ticket to bring you out to New York."

"Me?"

"Don't you want to come?"

"Is water wet?"

"Then all we have to do is pick a date and I'll take care of the ticket."

We settled on the Saturday after my finals in December. That way I could spend a whole week with Darwin and still be back in time for Christmas with my family.

"Besides," I added, "we have something to celebrate. I'm going to win that bet we made and you have to pay up."

CHAPTER THIRTY-TWO

Hook, Line, and Sinker

Thanksgiving morning we overslept. Mom was late for her appoint-ment. Theodore and I got stuck making pies and mashed potatoes. He complained so much while peeling potatoes that I let him watch the Thanksgiving Day parade on television while I made the pies—two pumpkin and two cherry. I hoped Mom would get back before I fin-ished. Pies were not what I did best. It took me three tries each to cover the bottom of the pie plates. They were reasonably patched together when I started on the filling for the pumpkin. We were out of allspice. Grandma Willis was busy making salads when I called her for help.

"This will be the first time in twenty years my family will be together for Thanksgiving," she said.

I sent Theodore to Grandma's house for the spice.

Unfortunately, Mom arrived just as I finished globbing the brown sugar topping on the cherry pies. It should have been crumbly, not globby.

"It will taste real good," she said as I put them in the oven. I was glad she didn't say any more.

We planned to eat around three o'clock. Mom didn't feel so nau-seated at that time of day, and Aunt Jean and Uncle Bill were coming from Beaver. It gave them plenty of time for the drive. As for me, Thanksgiving was a milestone putting me that much closer to New York. In less than three weeks I'd be back home.

"I have an announcement to make," Dad said, banging a spoon on his water glass. Aunt Jean and Mom stopped talking. Theodore used the diversion to shove his last piece of turkey onto Calvin's plate.

"I saw that," Calvin accused, dropping the piece back onto what remained of Theodore's potatoes and gravy.

"You touched it," Theodore complained. "It's yours now." He flipped it at Calvin, but the turkey landed on the floor.

"That's not funny!" Dad boomed. "Theodore get that turkey off of Grandma's carpet, NOW."

I looked at Spencer. "Kids are so immature." I figured whatever it was Dad was planning to announce would definitely be anticlimactic. I was wrong.

"As you know," Dad began, "coming back to Utah was a hard decision, but at Gloria's insistence, we're here." He smiled at Mom. "I want to thank her publicly for returning us to our roots. In the bright lights of New York, I had forgotten the most important things in life—namely my wife and children. To get back on the right track, Gloria and I have decided to be sealed in the temple."

Aunt Jean hugged and kissed them both. Tears streamed down Grandma's cheeks. I felt like crying, too, but not because I was thrilled like Grandma was. Mom and Dad had been hauled in hook, line, and sinker—they were traitors. Now our family would never be the same. They had slashed it to pieces. I pushed my chair back and stomped through the kitchen past my pies to the backyard. They would probably taste awful, anyway.

I sat in Grandma's swing, pushing angrily at the ground as it went higher. I was ostracized. Cut off. I kicked a twig and sent it skidding across the grass. Maybe when I finally got to New York, I wouldn't come back. Ever.

I don't know how long I sat there feeling sorry for myself with the cold breeze slapping at my face, but finally Dad came looking for me. He had a piece of my pumpkin pie.

"I don't want to help with the dishes," I barked. "And I don't want any of that awful pie." I wiped at my eyes trying to hide the signs of tears.

"What's wrong, Julie?" Dad asked. "Your pies are wonderful. I had a piece of each kind."

"It's not the pie," I said, staring at my dirt-covered shoes. "It's you and Mom."

"We thought you'd be pleased about us marrying in the temple."

"I'm not."

"When we stopped at Temple Square and talked about being a forever family, I thought you agreed."

I stared at the barren branches in the once-lush garden. "Nothing's forever. Everything changes. The trees are so barren they look dead."

"But they're not. Winter is just a hard time for them. Come spring, blossoms will grow and they'll bloom into even bigger trees than they are now."

Stopping the swing, I looked him squarely in the face, trying to let him see all the hurt and pain he was causing me. "I'm not a tree, Dad. I never will be."

He set the pie on a nearby garden chair and walked closer, putting his arms around me. I let him do it so he would know what he was throwing away.

"Oh, Julie, this is all my fault. If I hadn't been so willing to let business take up all my time, you would have grown up in the Church."

"And then I would have been brainwashed before I was eight just like everybody else," I said bitterly.

Dad stiffened and pulled away. "You're a young lady now. I can't make up your mind for you. I can only tell you why I made the decision I did."

As I looked at him, my mouth drooped. Say it and get it over with, I thought.

"I think your mother's illness is a blessing in disguise."

"How can you say that? She may die!" I exploded, turning my back on him.

"Heavens, Julie. I didn't say I was glad she was sick."

I brushed off his attempt to touch my shoulder.

"I love your mother. I want to be with her forever. Life is so short. I couldn't bear having her with me for only this lifetime, whether it's forty more years or only the next few months. Can you understand what I'm saying?"

"You're saying forever exists."

"It does, Julie. I know it now and I just wish you knew it, too."

I shrugged.

"Will you do me a favor?" he pleaded.

I didn't answer.

"Your Mom and I would like to get married in the temple in about two weeks. We would like to have you and Theodore sealed to us at the same time. Since you're both older than eight, you need to be baptized. Will you pray about it?"

I turned around and yelled at him. "So that's the solution to everything. Just pray and the answer will hit you over the head."

"Sometimes it works that way," he said softly. "Most of the time it's a lot harder."

"Well, I've prayed," I confided, "and I haven't been struck by lightning with an answer."

"Keep trying, Julie. Theodore wants to get baptized on Saturday."

Three traitors, I thought, as he walked away. I sacrificed Juilliard for you, I wanted to scream at his back.

I had been going to church every Sunday like a dutiful daughter, but I didn't have to believe. I didn't want to. Believing would make New York all glitter with no substance. That was my life for eighteen years. How could I give it up?

The back door slammed and Spencer walked around the corner of the house.

"How did you get out of washing dishes?" I asked.

"I didn't join in the food fight between Calvin and your brother."

"They started in again?"

"They're going to be washing until midnight." He walked behind the swing. "I wonder how high this thing can go?"

Spencer was nice, I thought, as he pushed me higher. Too bad everyone couldn't be like him.

CHAPTER THIRTY-THREE

Theodore Succumbs

Saturday arrived too soon. I sat on the back row, hoping Theodore's baptism would be short. I looked at my watch. If they didn't start soon, I'd miss the movie I wanted to watch on television.

I caught the bishop looking at me and then raising his eyebrows at Mom.

"She's not ready," I heard her whisper.

Joshua sat down on the chair next to me just as I was considering a long visit to the ladies room. He was all smiles, beaming like a kid on Christmas morning.

"What's wrong with you?" I snapped.

"I'm happy."

"We both are," Cindy said, slipping into the chair next to him. "Isn't it wonderful about Theodore?" she asked.

Theodore and who else? I thought, looking at them sitting so sweetly together.

The bishop started the meeting, and I stared straight ahead, wishing I were somewhere else, someplace like New York. New York was colder than Utah. I imagined Darwin and me ice skating in Central Park. I preferred the outdoor lake to the indoor rink at Rockefeller Center. The brisk air and laughter of the other skaters, the feel of strength as he pulled me along after him were memories from last year I wanted to relive again as soon as possible.

After we finished skating, we had gone to a small shop for coffee and donuts. I remembered the warmth and the stale odor of cigarettes. Would I drink coffee again once I was back with Darwin? I wasn't a Mormon, so there was no reason not to.

Suddenly Joshua's voice cut into my reverie. I was shocked to see him standing at the podium.

". . . and so, Theodore," Joshua said, "when you're confirmed a member of The Church of Jesus Christ of Latter-day Saints, you'll be given the gift of the Holy Ghost to guide you. If you listen, he'll warn you against danger and keep you on the right track."

So there was God, Jesus, and now this Casper character to sit on your shoulder and dictate what you should do. The idea of Casper following Theodore around was funny. As soon as I laughed, I regretted it. These people, no matter how misguided, truly believed in their church. Who was I to say they couldn't. They had their rights, too.

I sat sullenly through the rest of the meeting.

The following Saturday, Mom, Dad, and Theodore went to the temple. Since I didn't want to wait in the Visitors' Center for three hours, I stayed home. Let them go and do what they wanted. Then they would let me do what I wanted. Sitting down at Ruwanda, I tore into Beethoven's Fifth Symphony. The rise and fall of the music always lifted my spirits, but today, the classical stuff just didn't make me feel the way it used to.

I stared at the Church hymnbook a full minute before picking it up. It opened to page twenty six, "Joseph Smith's First Prayer." Amazing, they wrote a song about their prophet's first prayer. After playing it through, I sang a few bars.

The doorbell rang at the end of the first line.

"That wasn't classical music I heard coming up the steps," Joshua said.

"I'm trying to figure our how the song goes. Come in and you can sing it for me."

"Who, me?"

I tried to look exasperated.

". . . Joseph's humble prayer was answered, And he listened to the Lord.

Oh, what rapture filled his bosom, For he saw the living God: Oh, what rapture filled his bosom, For he saw the living God."

"Gee," I said when he finished, "you should go out for the opera."

"That good, huh?" Joshua grinned.

"As the prop man," I said.

"I'd like to, but I can't."

"You think the position might be taken?"

"No, I'm going on a trip."

"Where to?"

"New York." He sat down on the bench beside me.

"I'm going to New York, too. Maybe we'll see each other." I envisioned Darwin meeting Joshua. They were like two symphonies played in different keys. It would be interesting watching them try to harmonize.

"I'm going for two years, Julie."

"Are your parents moving?"

"No, I got my mission call."

"What!" His statement struck like the roll of tympani.

"I'm leaving the first week in January."

"What does Cindy think?" I stammered.

"I haven't told her yet." He took my hands in his and looked into my eyes. "Will you write to me?"

I sat there with my mouth open. I knew it was coming. He had told me it was. Suddenly it was very real and slapping me in the face.

"Why haven't you told Cindy?"

"We'll tell her now, if you want to."

"If I want to?" I sounded like a broken record.

"I wanted you to be the first to know."

"Why?"

"Because I care for you. There are so many things about you that are good. I don't want to lose touch while I'm gone. Even if you have a hundred other boyfriends, I still want to be counted as one." He smiled and then said in a serious tone. "This mission call is very important to me. It's what I've lived my life for. I want you to know that."

He stopped talking and touched my cheek.

153

I sighed. "I suppose there's nothing I can do to talk you out of it."

"Nothing."

"Well, then, do you want the letter on eating humble pie first or would you prefer something else?" I asked.

He pulled me to my feet and we walked outside to the swing. "What did you think about the words to that song?" he asked.

"I thought that was some answer for a first prayer."

"That wasn't the first time he prayed."

"But the title says . . ."

"Never mind what the title says. What the title means is that it was the first time he prayed aloud. You see, before he had only prayed silently to himself. You know, in his bed at night."

"With the covers pulled up to his chin?" I added.

"Something like that. Then Joseph Smith began to do a lot of reading in the Bible. In fact, it was a scripture in James that convinced him to seek a place to pray out loud. 'If any of you lack wisdom, let him ask of God, that giveth to all men liberally, and upbraideth not.'"

"What does *upbraideth* mean?"

"It means God won't hold back. All you have to do is ask sincerely and the Holy Ghost will cause a burning inside you and you'll know it's all true."

"Who, Casper?"

"The Holy Ghost isn't the same thing, Julie. You have to find out for yourself."

I sat silently for a minute. The thought of Mom, Dad, and Theodore all dressed in white came to mind. I felt like crying, but didn't know why. "Okay, so what do I have to do to find out?"

Joshua squeezed my hand. "You have to read the scriptures and you have to pray sincerely. If you want, we can pray together right now."

I closed my eyes. "Go ahead."

"Let's kneel down."

My eyes popped open. "Right here?"

We ended up kneeling beside the couch in the living room. When Joshua finished praying, I stood up. "Let's go get ice cream."

He pulled me back down. "Now it's your turn."

"Maybe God's too busy. You just bothered him with your prayer. He probably doesn't want to hear from me."

"Heavenly Father is never too busy to listen."

"Dear God," I prayed. "Joshua really believes in you and the Church and the Book of Mormon. He wants me to believe too." I opened one eye and looked at Joshua. "But I don't know if I really want to believe, because that would mean that I would have to give up . . . my a . . ."

"Pride," Joshua prompted.

"Pride," I said. "Excuse me a moment, God."

"Who's prayer is this anyway," I hissed at Joshua. "I don't want to give up my pride."

"Sorry. You're doing great." He pecked me on the cheek and bowed his head again.

"Like I was saying, God. I lived just fine without you for eighteen years. I'd like to continue that. Just don't send me any more problems and make my mother well. Thank you, Amen."

"Do you really believe God can make your mother well?" Joshua asked.

"Don't you?"

"Of course."

"Just one question. Are you doing all this to practice up for your mission?"

He smiled at me, his brown eyes sparkling behind horn-rimmed glasses; then he took my hand. We walked over to Cindy's house and the three of us went out for ice cream to celebrate Joshua's mission call.

CHAPTER THIRTY-FOUR

The Big Apple

Finals week left me bleary-eyed and anxious for my trip to New York. The thought of escape was rejuvenating as I left BYU campus. Tomorrow I would be back in the Big Apple. I even looked forward to seeing the Statue of Liberty. I had always taken the lady with the torch for granted, but now she symbolized freedom. I might even talk Darwin into taking the Staten Island Ferry, so I could salute her in person.

My plum-colored dress was the last thing packed. I was certain there would be a place to wear it in New York.

As I was zipping the bag closed, Theodore burst into the room waving an envelope in the air. "You got a letter from Elder Patience."

I grabbed it out of his hand.

"Open it," he pleaded.

I unzipped my suitcase a crack and stuffed it in.

"I will later," I said.

"Oh, please," he whined. "I want to tell Sam about his brother."

He bugged me all the way to the airport.

"Be good," Mom said as I hugged her good-bye.

"I will," I promised. Then I wished I hadn't. Good and fun could be opposites, each pulling in different directions. I didn't want one to get in the way of the other.

"Hi, babe," Darwin said, kissing me hard on the mouth, "I missed you so much."

Willing the moment to last forever, I clung to him, relishing the feeling of being in his arms again. The intensity of his masculinity had always made me feel vulnerable. I smiled at him and got a wolfish grin in return.

"You've changed," I said as we climbed in the car.

"For the better, I hope."

"I haven't decided yet."

"Where's your mom and dad?" I asked as we drove into the city.

"They're at a cocktail party. We're meeting them at Fiorella's later for dinner."

"Oh, how I miss this place," I sighed.

"It's missed you," he countered.

"Maybe I should stay and never go back."

"Promise."

I sighed again. "My mother's expecting me."

"How is she?"

I looked at the skyline. The twin towers suddenly seemed cold and distant. "She'll be finished with her treatment in another month."

"Great! Then you're moving back."

"I wish it were that easy. We still won't know if they got it all." I still couldn't bring myself to say the word *cancer*.

Sunday we got up late and took a tour of the city. Darwin's parents had been cordial enough the night before, but I was glad to get away. They had asked a lot of questions about Dad's business and what kind of place we were living in now. I felt uncomfortable stretching the truth.

At my insistence we took the Staten Island Ferry.

"Let's look over the rail," I said, pushing on the door leading to an outside deck.

"It's freezing out there," Darwin warned.

"Stay here then. I'll only be a minute."

He stood near the door as I walked to the rail. The freezing air hit in blasts as the ferry slowly bucked the waves. Gray clouds were gathering on the horizon. I reached the rail and winked at the Statue of

Liberty. Freedom to do what I want. Looking down at the water churning out from under the boat, I stood mesmerized. Finally my gloved fingers clutching the rail were as numb as my nose. I looked back at Darwin.

"Cold enough for you?" he asked, opening the door for me.

My head nodded of its own accord.

"Let's get something hot."

He led me to a small concession stand.

"Two coffees," he said.

I took mine and followed him to an empty bench.

"Too hot?" he asked, taking my cup and blowing on it.

I took a sip. The bitter liquid burned a path down my throat. Why had I missed drinking this stuff so much?

"Do they have cream and sugar?" I asked.

"I thought you liked it black."

"Not any more."

The added ingredients only made it sickly sweet. I used it to warm my fingers and stared out the water-spotted window. The storm was getting worse.

"So tell me about Utah," Darwin said, draining his cup and pulling me close. "How's the skiing?"

"I guess it's pretty good."

"You haven't tried it?"

"I've been busy with school. And I usually take Mom to the hospital on Saturdays."

"You sound homesick," he teased.

"I do not," I insisted. "Besides, a bet's a bet and you lost."

"Not until January first."

"I've already decided. I'm never joining that Church. You may as well pay up now."

Hail suddenly lashed against the windows. The pale winter sun was hidden behind its onslaught.

The ferry arrived late. We stayed on board to await the return trip. Sunday turned out to be a dark and dreary day.

On Monday I went to New York University with Darwin. He still had two more days of classes. I walked around the library while he took two exams. Four hours later, I saw him coming and started toward him. A blond in a smart-looking fur coat beat me to him. She was kissing him when my eyes met Darwin's.

Prying her arms from his neck, he slowly turned her around. "Kim, this is Julie; Julie, Kim."

He could have spared us both the introduction. Kim's eyes narrowed to slits and she hung possessively to Darwin's arm.

"I see you're busy," I said, turning away and walking toward the nearest exit.

Darwin caught me as I headed down the steps. "Julie," he said grabbing my arm.

Kim walked past us, a pout on her face.

I jerked my arm away from Darwin. "What have you been up to?" I scolded. "You haven't been sitting home alone on Friday nights, have you?"

"And neither have you."

"What makes you so sure?"

"Because you're too pretty."

He certainly had a way of manipulating the situation to his advantage. Now I shared the guilt.

He spun me around. "Look, Julie, it doesn't matter what we do when we're apart. What matters is that we're together now. We need to make the most of today and forget about yesterday or even what may happen tomorrow. I don't want you to stay angry at me. Our time together is too short." He cupped my face in his hands. "I love you too much," he said, kissing me on the forehead, then the nose and then the mouth.

It was the same place he had just kissed Kim. I pulled away from him. "What about *her*?"

"Kim's in the Ski Club. I've seen her on the slopes a few times. That's all."

"And Francine?" I asked, dreading the answer.

Darwin laughed. "Francine got back together with Dave at Thanksgiving. I'm sorry I forgot to mention it."

I didn't go to the university with Darwin the next day. I took the bus to Trump Towers instead.

"Hey, Alfred," I called to the guard in front of the Resident's

Lobby. When he turned around, I didn't recognize him.

"Is this Alfred's day off?"

"Alfred who?" the new guard asked.

"Sorry, forget it."

I shoved my hands in my pockets and walked around to the main entrance. The place was as busy as ever and I flowed in with the crowd. Taking the escalator up, I walked slowly past the shop windows. Everything was geared for Christmas. Mink coats and fox-tail furs were surrounded by elves and fairy lights. High-top boots, midlength wool skirts, and a variety of elegant sweaters were displayed against a background of sparkling snow. A miniature train wound its way among the merchandise. I walked into a shop on the third floor and tried on a designer cashmere pullover. Everything fit perfectly, except the price. "Wrong color," I told the sales clerk.

Leaving quickly, I rode the escalator higher to the outdoor garden. The door was jammed. I rammed it with my shoulder.

"Are you trying to break the glass?" a waiter from a nearby restaurant asked.

"Why doesn't it open? It's always open."

"Where have you been? We're having an energy crisis. The door's been locked for over a month."

I walked to the inside rail and leaned over, watching the water plummet to the lobby. At least the four-story cascade was still as beautiful as ever. Only it didn't compare to Bridal Veil Falls. The natural waterfall in Provo Canyon was twice the height, tumbling gently onto black rocks. I wondered what it would look like in winter with snow on the ground. I would have to drive up there with Joshua and Cindy when I got back.

What an awful thought, wishing I were back in Utah. I went down to the lobby and out onto the street. I bought a hot pretzel dotted with mustard. I was in New York having a good time . . . and freezing to death. A wind flurry burst around the corner carrying bits of ice and snow. It stung my cheeks and clung to my hair. I gobbled the pretzel down so fast I choked on the mustard. At least now I could stick my hands into my pockets. I still had two blocks to walk to get to my bus stop, and there wasn't an empty taxi in sight.

CHAPTER THIRTY-FIVE

Losing the Bet

The weather, though bitter cold, hadn't been cold enough long enough to freeze the lake in Central Park solid for ice skating. With the rink at Rockefeller Center closed for maintenance, ice skating was out of the question. I suggested we try the ballet at Lincoln Center instead. Because of the holiday season, the only seats left were on the back row. We went anyway.

"I should have brought my father's binoculars," Darwin complained.

I sat silently watching the fly specks leap across the stage.

"The music was good," I said afterwards.

"The dancing probably was too," Darwin chuckled.

Over pasta and a Sprite, Darwin suddenly asked, "So who is he? The guy you've been going out with." I choked on my drink.

"What makes you think . . . ?"

"Julie, it's obvious you're thinking of someone else half the time. Now who is he? I want to know something about the competition."

I stared at my plate. A few days ago Darwin had told me to live for the moment, forgetting the past, disregarding the future. In reality, he was as curious as I was. "Well," I hesitated, "there is this one guy who helps me with my religion homework."

"And?"

I looked up. "And if you're dying to meet him, you can. He's moving out to New York the first of January. I'll give him your address. I'm sure he'd like to stop by for a chat."

"What's his name?" Darwin asked.

"His first name?"

"And his last."

"Elder," I said. "Elder Peterson."

"What makes you so sure Elder wants to talk to me?"

"He's very friendly. If you ask him, he'll come back five or six times."

Darwin scratched his head. "What's he moving to New York for?"

"Two years," I said, avoiding the truth.

"Is there some sort of business course he's taking out here?"

"Something like that." I started choking again and managed to change the subject.

That night I dreamed about Walt Disney's *Fantasia*. Music from Beethoven's "Pastoral Symphony" played softly as winged horses swooped and soared through the fountains and clouds of their mystical land. Suddenly, the pounding beat of Igor Stravinsky's "The Rite of Spring" began to overlay Beethoven's melody. The winged horses flew from their resplendent fairy-tale garden into the desert skies of the prehistoric past. They swooped and soared after the giant plant-eaters, teasing the dinosaurs and nipping at their tails. From the depths of a nearby canyon roared a tyrannosaurus, snapping with massive teeth and clawing the air as the chargers winged toward him. I woke in a cold sweat.

Two symphonies, I thought, played in different keys. Why not? I lay there trying to come up with a way to make another bet. One that Darwin couldn't refuse. The irony of the situation hit me toward dawn. What about the first bet? Was I really sure I wanted to win?

On Saturday afternoon, we accompanied Darwin's parents to a special Christmas program. It was the one time a year they attended church together. Paid professionals were presenting the story of the birth of Christ with excerpts from the *Messiah*. The music alone sounded promising enough.

Even in my plum-colored marvel I felt *under*dressed as I walked down the isle, and the cathedral was incredible. Gothic archways led to a high vaulted ceiling, decorated with ancient Christian art. A carving of Christ hung on a cross directly in front. At his feet was an ornate golden altar.

The congregation stood when the priest entered the assembly hall. His long flowing robes, neck band, and chain gave him a regal appearance. Instead of a crown, however, he wore a high headdress that matched the gold in his robe.

He began reading a letter with beautifully phrased thoughts praising God. As his speech continued I noticed everyone had their heads bowed.

"What's going on?" I nudged Darwin.

"This is the prayer," he whispered.

Prayer? He's reading it off a paper! Joshua had said that prayer came from the heart. As I stared at the priest, he turned the page. It must have taken several days to write.

When I nudged Darwin again, he took a book from the back of the seat in front of us and put it on my lap. "There's any prayer you'll ever need right here."

I was flipping through the pages when the singing started. The music and blending of voices was superb. Spellbound, I left the open book on my lap and watched the director. Slowly it dawned on me that I didn't understand the words.

"What are they saying?" I whispered to Darwin.

He shrugged. "It's in Latin."

"Do you understand it?"

He chuckled softly. "Latin's a dead language. Nobody does."

"Not even the priest?"

Darwin considered that. "He probably does."

My thrill over the music was dampened, and I began making comparisons to my grandparents' ward in Provo. The building in Utah was simple, built as a place of learning and worship. It was a place where the members edified one another with their humble testimonies.

The cathedral, on the other hand, seemed an elaborately decorated hull The music resounded from the walls, yet I felt hollow and empty.

My goodnight to Darwin was brief. I hurried to my room, locking the door behind me. After dressing for bed, I dug Benjamin's letter out of the bottom of the suitcase and sat down to read it.

Dear Julie,

This is probably the last letter I will be able to write before I come home in January. Things have been really hectic here. I don't have enough hours in the day to get it all done.

Our mission hit its record high in baptisms this last month. Imagine the joy of having so many people embrace the gospel truths in the same month.

We are planning a Christmas Eve fireside for all the missionaries. My assignment is to prepare a talk on what Christ has done for us. I know he lives and that he is my personal Savior. True happiness comes only from following him. What I feel in my heart, I know I won't be able to cram into fifteen minutes.

Christ is there for you, too. All you have to do is knock.

Have a Merry Christmas and a Happy New Year.

Elder Ben Patience

A tear fell on Benjamin's name, smearing it beyond recognition. I wiped my eyes and slid off the bed. Kneeling down just as Joshua and I had a few days ago, I buried my head in my hands.

"Okay, God," I said out loud. "I think I'm ready to listen."

I thought about Brother Van Horn and his lesson on faith. Planting watermelon seeds in class was the craziest thing I'd ever seen. I don't know who was more surprised, Grandpa or me, to find a tiny watermelon growing among the pansies by the front porch. "Help me to have faith," I pleaded, "and help it to grow."

I thought about Spencer with his matter-of-fact attitude about going on a mission and Theodore's baptism with the light shining from his eyes. I had denied it then, but I could see it clearly now. Theodore had tried to be good as much as I had tried to aggravate him in the past week. I hadn't even let him read Benjamin's letter. Another tear landed on the bedspread. I brushed it away.

"Help me to be kind to Theodore and forgive my impatience with him."

I reflected on the conversation my father and I had held under the grapevines. The Wasatch Front he had said; he would climb the Wasatch Front to have his family with him forever. So far, I hadn't even been willing to step off the front porch.

"Please soften my heart to accept the truth," I prayed.

The image of Freddy, standing to fight for home and family as Captain Moroni came to mind. "Thank you for Freddy."

"And thank you for Joshua," I prayed. "He believes in me even more than I do. Forgive me and help me to be strong like him."

Suddenly I imagined Mom lying in a hospital bed, an IV attached to her arm, a breathing apparatus taped to her face.

"She's dying," I heard the doctor say.

No, please No!

I reached for her, but she faded slowly from view. I wept, my face cradled in my hands. It's my fault she's gone. I'll never see her again.

After what seemed like forever, I dried my eyes and looked around the room. Everything was the same as it had been when I started praying, but now it seemed unreal. The pain I was feeling inside was reality.

Closing my eyes, I prayed again. "Please, God. Don't let my mother die because of me. You can make her whole. Joshua believes you can . . . and I believe it too."

That night I had the strangest dream. I saw my family standing outside the temple dressed in white. They were beckoning for me to join them. As I walked closer, I felt happy and warm.

CHAPTER THIRTY-SIX

The Second Bet

"Ready for the ski slopes?" Darwin asked me at breakfast.

I frowned. "I was thinking we might try something else today, something we've never done together before."

Darwin poured us each a bowl of corn flakes. "Shoot."

"Since it's Sunday, I thought we could go to church."

He looked at me, his blue eyes wide. "Church?"

"It doesn't take up too much of the day," I apologized.

"We went to church last night." He sounded annoyed. "Why do you want to go again?"

"It was just an idea," I said, starting to back down. He passed me the pitcher and crunched a mouthful of flakes. As I poured the milk, I thought: you either know or you don't. It's either true or it isn't. You can't sit in the middle allowing yourself to be blown from side to side.

"Julie!" Darwin yelled. "That's enough."

Several flakes floated over the edge of the bowl in a puddle of milk.

"Okay," he said as I sponged it up. "If you really want to go, I'll call the cathedral and find out what time the service is."

"The cathedral! Not your church, the Mormon Church."

Darwin's laugh sounded like a braying donkey. "This is a joke, right? What about winning the bet? You already told me I lost."

"I've changed my mind. You win."

"Just like that, no explanation?"

I put the sponge down and looked at him. "I know it's true."

Two hours later, we pulled into the underground parking lot of a multistory building. "Julie, how can you know something is true without scientific proof?" Darwin asked.

"I feel it inside."

"So this whole thing is based on feelings. What if you feel differently tomorrow?"

"I won't."

"How can you know for sure?"

"I prayed about it."

He got out of the car and slammed the door.

We rode the elevator to the third floor.

"Whoever heard of a church in an office building, anyway," he grumbled.

"You didn't have to come."

"It's our last day together." He softened and took my hand.

The third floor was immense, one chapel to the right and one to the left. Sacrament meeting was just starting in the one on the left. We walked in that direction.

"It's modern," Darwin conceded, looking around.

I'd never seen a chapel in an office building, either. If I hadn't called for directions, we wouldn't have found it.

"Who's that?" Darwin whispered when a man wearing a business suit stood up to conduct.

"That's the bishop."

"Where's the priest?"

I shrugged.

What surprised Darwin the most, however, was when the twelve-year-old boys passed the sacrament.

"They don't even shave, yet," he complained.

"They're deacons," I explained.

It was a good meeting. The Spirit was strong. I kept sneaking glances at Darwin, trying to read his thoughts.

"Amen," Darwin said a little too loudly after the closing prayer. He started to stand up. I pulled him back down.

"That's just the end of the *first* meeting."

He frowned. "How many more are there?"

"Only two."

"Two!" He loosened his tie and sighed.

"The time will fly by," I promised.

"Well, what did you think?" I asked, when we were back in the car. Darwin smiled for the first time that morning. "No wonder they got you."

"What do you mean by that?"

"They're very convincing."

"How convincing?"

"Not enough for me to alter my lifestyle, but I can see how someone else might succumb." He winked at me and I hit him.

"I'll bet if you went to church as many times as I have, you'd be converted."

"No way. I like being my own man, and I don't need the shackles of religion dragging me down."

"Up," I corrected.

"I don't need change," he said, starting the car.

I waved to some of the new friends we'd met as we drove out of the parking lot.

"Let's make it double or nothing," I challenged.

"If you're talking about the bet, I've already won. You said so yourself this morning."

"Not if I wait until January to get baptized."

Darwin laughed. "You're devious. How did they ever get you?"

"That's what I want you to find out."

"Don't do this to me, Julie," Darwin warned. When he looked at me, I knew he was on the verge of wavering.

"We'll make it simple," I said, taking his hand. "I'll bet that you can't listen to the missionary discussions without joining the Church."

"How many are there?"

"Six."

"So all I have to do is listen to six lessons?"

I squeezed his hand. I knew I had him. "One hour a week for six weeks."

Darwin snickered. "That's too easy."

"Then it's a bet?"

"You're on."

I hugged him and the car swerved. "You won't regret this."

"I think I already do."

CHAPTER THIRTY-SEVEN

The Referral

"... I baptize you in the name of the Father, and of the Son, and of the Holy Ghost," Joshua said. The water swirled over me as he pushed me under.

I felt myself being lifted up and knew I had made it. I was a soaking wet, new member of The Church of Jesus Christ of Latter-day Saints.

I could hear my friends and family singing "O My Father" and "Joseph Smith's First Prayer" as I changed into dry clothes. When they finished, my father laid his hands on my head and gave me the gift of the Holy Ghost. I smiled at the bishop. In fact, I smiled at everyone in the room. The only one with a bigger smile was my mother.

That night we set the second Saturday in January as a sealing date. I was going to be with my family for eternity. Of course, that would mean Theodore would be around forever. I looked at Theodore and sighed. It wouldn't take him that long to grow up, would it?

The day after New Year's, Joshua left on his mission. I rode with Cindy to the airport to see him off.

"This is an exciting day," she said.

"I think it's depressing," I countered.

"Hey, I'll miss him, too." She patted my knee. "But missions are inevitable. They turn boys into men. It's the discipline and living close to the Spirit. They come home spiritual giants."

Would Joshua come home more of a spiritual giant than he already was? "Where did you hear that from?" I asked.

"It's public knowledge. Benjamin will be home in two weeks, then you'll see."

Maybe I would at that.

We found Joshua in the lobby waiting for his flight. I walked up behind him and tapped him on the shoulder.

"Hey, Elder," I said.

When he turned, I saw a light in his eyes I hadn't noticed before.

"Good luck," I said, blinking back the tears.

He shook my hand. "See you in two years. Don't forget to write."

"I think I've still got a copy of that letter on humility."

"My favorite subject," he joked.

He would have said more, but his family was there. It was a difficult occasion, one of joy mingled with melancholy. He turned to Cindy and then back to his mother and father. I watched him clown around with his brothers and sisters. The high spirits covered a deeper feeling of sadness at separation. Would leaving home and family be worth the results? I hoped Cindy was right.

"Flight 214 now boarding for New York," the intercom droned.

"Got to go," Joshua said. He came full circle back to me. "You make a great Mormon, Julie."

"Be a good missionary, Joshua," I replied. I pressed an envelope into his hand. "This is your first referral."

"Who is it?" he asked.

"I'll bet you can't baptize him," I challenged.

About the Author

Chirley Roundy Arnold loves adventure, far away places, and the young women of the Church. She has been on safari in Kenya, waded in the Dead Sea in Israel, climbed the Eiffel Tower in France and scaled the leaning tower of Pisa in Italy. Over the past eighteen years Chirley has lived in Africa and Latin America. She speaks Spanish and French fluently and has visited more than thirty-four countries as a diplomat's wife.

Chirley has been a ward and stake Young Women's leader and a seminary teacher. She has also volunteered as a Girl Scout leader, Suzuki violin teacher, square dance instructor, and softball and basketball coach for both young men and women.

She has published articles in the *Church News* and international magazines of the Church about members living in Mali and the Ivory Coast.

Chirley recently moved from Centreville, Virginia, to Moscow, Russia, with her husband and six children.